DO N
B
BEGI

ARE YOU READY FOR THE ULTIMATE CHALLENGE?

It's a whole new way to GIVE YOURSELF GOOSEBUMPS. There's only *one way out*! If you don't make all the right moves — in the right order — you'll never see the light of day again.

Here's the deal: You went on a class trip to the Hall of Science. When the rest of the class left, you stayed behind to finish a video game. Bad idea. Because now an evil Super Computer doesn't want you to leave — ever!

You're in deep trouble. The hall is full of dangers. Like a deadly Mirror Maze. A giant, thirsty mosquito. And a flock of model dinosaurs with very sharp teeth!

And remember, there's only one way out. Make one mistake — and you're history.

NOW, GET READY TO TAKE THE ULTIMATE CHALLENGE!

[Look for the solution in the back of Give Yourself Goosebumps #27: *Checkout Time at the Dead-end Hotel.*]

READER BEWARE —
YOU CHOOSE THE SCARE!

Look for more
GIVE YOURSELF GOOSEBUMPS adventures
from R.L. STINE:

#1 Escape from the Carnival of Horrors
#2 Tick Tock, You're Dead!
#3 Trapped in Bat Wing Hall
#4 The Deadly Experiments of Dr. Eeek
#5 Night in Werewolf Woods
#6 Beware of the Purple Peanut Butter
#7 Under the Magician's Spell
#8 The Curse of the Creeping Coffin
#9 The Knight in Screaming Armor
#10 Diary of a Mad Mummy
#11 Deep in the Jungle of Doom
#12 Welcome to the Wicked Wax Museum
#13 Scream of the Evil Genie
#14 The Creepy Creations of Professor Shock
#15 Please Don't Feed the Vampire!
#16 Secret Agent Grandma
#17 Little Comic Shop of Horrors
#18 Attack of the Beastly Baby-sitter
#19 Escape from Camp Run-for-Your-Life
#20 Toy Terror: Batteries Included
#21 The Twisted Tale of Tiki Island
#22 Return to the Carnival of Horrors
#23 Zapped in Space
#24 Lost in Stinkeye Swamp
#25 Shop Till You Drop . . . Dead!

R.L. STINE

GIVE YOURSELF Goosebumps®

SPECIAL EDITION #1
THE ULTIMATE CHALLENGE: INTO THE JAWS OF DOOM

AN
APPLE
PAPERBACK

SCHOLASTIC INC.
New York Toronto London Auckland Sydney

A PARACHUTE PRESS BOOK

ISBN 0-590-39777-X

12 11 10 9 8 7 6 5 4 3 2 8 9/9 0 1 2 3/0

Printed in the U.S.A. 40

First Scholastic printing, February 1998

GAME OVER!

"No!" You slam your fist on the table as the words scroll across the computer screen. You lost again!

But you're getting better. I almost made it to level five that time, you congratulate yourself.

This class trip to the Hall of Incredible Science is much better than being in school. You figured a museum would be boring. But the hall is full of all kinds of gadgets, nature displays, and other cool stuff. The best part is the Thinking Machines Room. It's got incredible video games — including one based on your favorite movie of all time, *Operation Buzzard.*

They just announced that it's time for the bus to take you back to school. Most of your class has already headed downstairs. But you can't resist playing one more game.

You punch the START button. You hear the opening notes. A jungle scene appears in front of you.

Suddenly the screen goes blank.

Huh? Did the computer crash?

Then a message appears on the screen.

"Help me! The Super Computer has taken over!"

"What?" you mutter. Is one of the other kids from your class playing some kind of joke on you?

You glance around. There's no one else in the room.

Oh, well. You have to go anyway.

You leave the room and step into the open elevator.

But when the doors slide shut, it doesn't move.

You punch the buttons. You punch the buttons again.

Nothing happens.

You're trapped!

Don't panic, you tell yourself. You grab the emergency phone. "Hello? Hello?" you shout into the receiver.

A strange, deep voice answers. "You have learned my secret. Now you cannot leave the Hall of Incredible Science alive!"

"What secret?" you gasp. "Who are you?"

"I am the Super Computer," the voice declares. "I have taken over this entire building. But since you got that message, you know too much. Now you must be destroyed!"

"Wait!" you plead. "I thought that message was just a joke. I won't tell anyone. I promise!"

The voice just laughs.

Then the elevator jolts into motion.

You have a feeling you won't like where it's taking you.

INSTRUCTIONS

You are *so* doomed.

You're trapped in the Hall of Incredible Science. An evil computer has taken over, and you know its secret. Now it wants to silence you — forever.

The hall is filled with dangers. Every exhibit has been turned into a deadly menace. Even the building itself is out to get you!

There's only *one* way to get out of the building. To find it, you'll have to make all the right choices. Make a single mistake — and you'll never see the light of day again!

Let's face it. You probably won't last five minutes.

But just to make it interesting, turn the page for a few tips. If you read them carefully, you might just survive long enough to amuse the Super Computer before you're destroyed.

Of course, you might make it even madder. . . .

LEAVE NO STONE UNTURNED

The hall is full of deadly puzzles that you'll have to solve. Explore every room of the hall carefully. Remembering what you've seen will help you put the pieces together.

You may want to keep track of where you've gone. Each floor of the hall has a map that you should try to find. The maps have clues to help you figure out how to escape that floor.

You may also get some help from the "friend" who sent you the message. But your mystery pal is no match for the Super Computer.

INVENTORY

As you play, you'll have the opportunity to pick up useful gadgets, weapons, and other objects. When you pick up an object, write it down on the inventory list on page x.

But decide carefully before adding an object to your list. Remember, not everything in the Hall of Incredible Science is safe to play with! An object might be useful in one situation, but in another, it could lead to a sticky end. And some objects will just get you in trouble, no matter what you do with them.

Remember, too, that you may need certain objects in order to get other objects. This means you might have to explore a room more than once in order to get what you need.

FOLLOW THE NUMBERS

There are 238 numbered sections in the book. Begin with # 1. Then choose where to go next. Follow the directions at the end of each section. You will usually have several choices about what to do.

DO YOU FEEL LUCKY?

You'll also need a pair of dice. Sometimes, fighting a battle or doing something tricky will require that you roll a certain number. For example, an instruction might read:

Will you make it across the elevator shaft?
Roll to find out.
If you roll 8 or higher, go to # ***32****.*
If you roll 7 or lower, go to # ***164****.*

Roll the two dice. If they add up to 8 or higher, go to # ***32****. If they add up to 7 or lower, go to #* ***164****.*

That's all the advice you get. Not that it'll help. Oh, just one more thing: Don't forget to GIVE YOURSELF GOOSEBUMPS!

INVENTORY LIST

Write down on this page all the gadgets and objects you collect. Erase them or cross them out if you lose them.

#1

The elevator finally stops on the top floor of the Hall of Incredible Science. The doors slide open. You step out and immediately the doors whiz shut behind you. You gaze around.

There's no one here. The whole hall must be empty by now. But the back of your neck prickles. You can feel an evil presence watching you.

How are you going to escape?

---

*Try the elevator again? Turn to # **131**.*
*Try to find a telephone? Turn to # **89**.*

#2

Noise bomb in one hand, you fling open the doors.

The Visible Man bursts through. You throw the noise bomb.

KABOOOOM!

You clutch your ears in pain. You can't hear a thing!

As you dash for the door, you hope the Visible Man is too startled to stop you.

But you feel his slimy grip on your throat.

Guess the surprise is on you!

GAME OVER

#3

You dash back toward the dinosaur.

It plants itself in your path, rearing back in a silent roar. You decide to slide between its legs.

You shoot across the marble floor of the museum. The skeleton searches the floor behind you. It's not very smart!

With a few more steps, you reach the doors and bolt into the safety of the stairwell.

You made it!

---

*Turn to # **212**.*

#4

You head south and stumble out of the Maze of Mirrors.

This is the way you came in!

It takes a while for the dizziness to go away. All those reflecting images — so confusing!

From here, you can leave the Waves and Motion Room and head back into the main part of this floor.

Either that, or brave the maze again.

---

*Leave the Waves and Motion Room? Turn to # **194**.*

If you want to enter the Maze of Mirrors, check to see if you have the compass.

*The maze again, with the compass? Turn to # **138**.*

*The maze again, with no compass? Turn to # **75**.*

#5

You stretch your arm into the depths of the machine.

Got it!

As you pull the little computer out, it pings in your hand. Is it thanking you?

You free your hand and turn off the electric motor. These old calculators sure made a racket!

The tiny computer has a screen about four inches across. You stare intently at it.

Your jaw drops as you read what's printed there.

Turn to # ***105****.*

#6

You decide to head west.

You count thirty paces, then the hall turns north.

You walk another thirty paces that way, then reach a junction.

You can go east or further north.

Which way do you want to go?

East? Turn to # ***230****.*
North? Turn to # ***100****.*

#7

But as you dash past the Visible Man, his hand darts out. He grabs your wrist. The warm, slithery feeling of exposed muscles and veins makes you shudder.

He grips your other wrist. You're helpless in his slimy clutches.

Then he gazes at you with his lidless eyes and croaks out two words from his visible voice box:

"GAME OVER!"

#8

You try to squash the ants, smacking yourself all over. But more and more of them swarm on you.

You can't stand it. You jump to your feet to run away.

But as you stand, you feel dizzy. As if you were about to faint. Just as you black out, you spot another sign below the fire ants' destroyed case:

HANDLE WITH CARE. POISONOUS!

Guess you couldn't have *ant*-icipated that!

GAME OVER

#9

You level the laser and fire at one of the tiny monsters.

But the red beam just bounces off the solar panel on the little dinosaur's head. The beast starts moving faster!

You realize that you've made a bad mistake. These dinos are solar-powered. They eat light for breakfast!

Their gnashing teeth crackle with energy.

"Yikes!" you shout. You turn to run.

Turn to # ***137***.

#10

You grasp the controls. Your hands are slick with sweat.

The runway comes up to meet you. You're going to make it!

But then the Super Computer laughs. "Forgot about your landing gear, didn't you? Ha, ha, ha!"

Landing gear?

A screaming metal sound echoes through the cockpit. It's as if the bottom of your plane is tearing open on the runway.

But this isn't real, is it?

Maybe not. But try telling that to the crew that has to scrape you off the runway!

GAME OVER

#11

"Good work!" Peedee A. responds. "You're getting closer to me. But you'll need an electric motor to help me. Over and out."

You step carefully over the motionless dinosaurs and glance around the room. Everything is lit by the shaky lightning of the Tesla coil. It's spooky.

You have a feeling you'll find the electric motor here. But where should you look? Should you check out the Tesla coil or the electric toys?

The Tesla coil? Turn to # ***191***.
The electric toys? Turn to # ***74***.
Leave the Electricity Room? Turn to # ***13***.

#12

You steer back toward the runway. The airport appears in front of you. This looks so real, you think.

"Fire in Number Four engine," the voice announces.

The simulator shakes harder and harder. *BONK!* Ouch! That was your head hitting the ceiling. You're tossed around violently.

You've got to keep from crashing!

But what do you know about flying a plane?

Can you land the plane? Roll to find out.
If you roll 7 or higher, go to # ***10***.
If you roll 6 or lower, go to # ***174***.

#13

You're about to leave the Electricity Room when you notice something different about it.

It's not as dark as it was.

The giant lightbulb is slowly coming back on!

You realize that the switch must just turn it off for a few moments, to let it cool down. . . .

The little dinosaurs are starting to come back to life!

Oh, no. Run for it!

Can you make it to the door? Roll to find out.

*If you roll 9 or higher, go to # **116**.*

*If you roll 8 or lower, go to # **197**.*

#14

You spray the snake with your extinguisher. It hisses angrily as the cold gas plays across it.

But when you're done, the extinguisher has had no effect!

Except that the snake is madder than ever.

What should you try now? Take a look at your inventory list and choose a weapon.

---

*The space glove? Turn to # **144**.*

*A stink bomb? Turn to # **111**.*

*A noise bomb? Turn to # **198**.*

*Slink back out of the room? Turn to # **136**.*

#15

You struggle to yank the jet pack off the suit.

But there are so many clips and straps and buckles. And the space glove on your hand isn't helping.

The robot arm is dragging itself closer and closer. . . .

Maybe the space glove is making you too clumsy to unstrap the jet pack.

Should you throw it away? Or hang on to it?

Throw the space glove away? Turn to # ***226****.* *And cross* Space Glove *off your inventory list.*

Hang on and keep trying to unstrap the jet pack? Turn to # ***22****.*

#16

You pull on the gloves and set the visor over your eyes.

For a moment, you can't see anything.

Then, as you flex your fingers, sounds start to come from the little speakers in the helmet. Images begin forming in the blackness.

You gasp as a world appears around you.

Turn to # ***124****.*

#17

You decide to go for the key. You give the case a hard kick.

CRASH! Sand and ants tumble out onto the floor.

"Sorry, ants!" you apologize. They don't look happy.

In fact, as you sift through the sand for the key, the angry little creatures swarm all over you!

"Ouch!" you shout. One bit you!

You'd better do something about these ants.

---

*Swat them? Turn to # **8**.*

*Do you have the fire extinguisher? Turn to # **162**.*

#18

"Two. One. Liftoff!" the voice declares.

The capsule rumbles and shakes. You grip your seat tightly. You crash right through the ceiling into the rooftop atrium, where the cafeteria is. Finally the thundering noise stops.

You glance out the window — and gasp.

The cafeteria is swarming with spiderlike aliens!

It turns out that the Hall of Incredible Science is a giant intelligence test run by aliens. You passed!

That means your brain is good enough to eat.

Which they do. Yum!

GAME OVER

#19

"To escape, you'll have to defeat the Super Computer," Peedee A. continues.

This is too weird! "How do I do that?" you ask.

"First, you'll have to get down to the second floor. That's where I am. But don't use the elevators," Peedee A. warns. "The Super Computer controls them. It controls the whole building."

"Great," you moan. It's as if the biggest bully in school is out to get you. Times a million!

---

*Turn to # **97**.*

#20

You decide to follow the swooshing sound.

Whatever it is, it can't be any worse than what you've already seen in this terrifying place.

Can it?

You walk about twenty paces west, then south for thirty.

You come into a room with a giant pendulum swinging back and forth. But there's something funny about it. . . .

You take a closer look — and let out a scream!

---

*Turn to # **167**.*

#21

You race for the door to the fire stairs. The mosquito buzzes hungrily behind you. But you're going to make it!

You grab the door handle. *ZAAAAAP!*

"Oh, no!" you scream. This door is electrified! It feels as if you're being struck by lightning. And you can't let go!

Can you pry yourself loose before you are electrocuted? Roll the dice to find out.

If you roll 8 or higher, turn to # ***33***.
If you roll 7 or lower, turn to # ***121***.

#22

"Come on," you mutter at the jet pack. The screech of the robot arm dragging itself toward you sends shivers up your spine.

You yank desperately on a clamp.

HISSSSSSS!

You jump back. You've started up the jet pack! The space suit shoots toward the ceiling.

Your heart sinks as you watch the suit zoom off without you. Then a cold metal claw grips your throat.

This robot arm is a real pain in the neck!

GAME OVER

(Here's a hint: You need the boomerang to beat the robot arm. The boomerang is somewhere on this floor.)

#23

This is the second-floor map. Someone has spray-painted on it in bloodred letters. You gulp as you read the words.

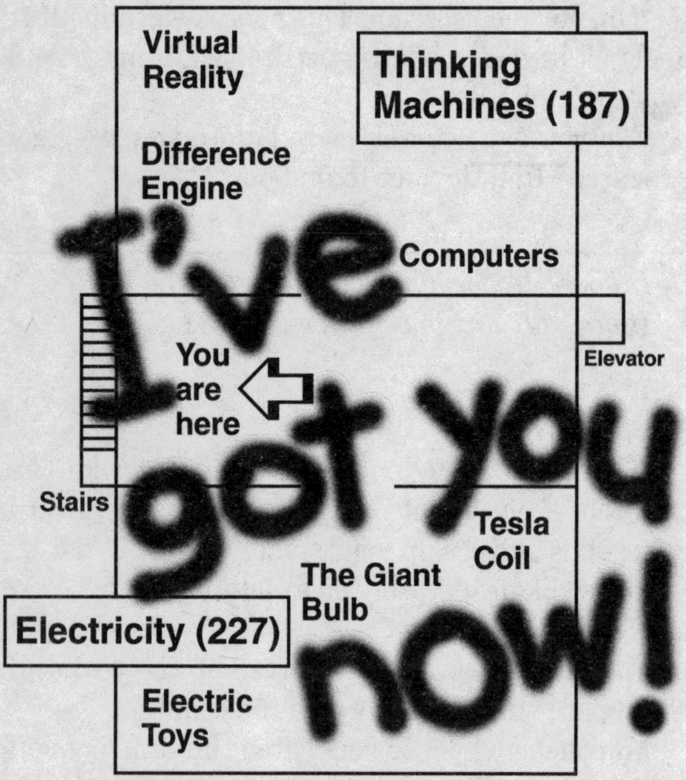

Write down "MAP OF 2nd FLOOR AT # 23." When you come here to glance at the map, make sure to remember where you came from.

If this is your first time here, turn to # ***161****.*

#24

Another voice takes its place.

An evil voice. One that has become all too familiar.

"You may have survived this time," the Super Computer taunts. "But I'll have the last laugh!"

"Not a chance, you bucket of bolts," you shout defiantly.

But you realize you have a lot further to go.

Where to now?

Check out the models? Turn to # ***91****.*

Leave the Aerodynamics Room? Turn to # ***166****.*

#25

You decide to go north.

But after only a few steps, your compass goes crazy!

The needle is spinning around and around. What now?

You feel yourself being tugged forward, as if an invisible hand were pulling you.

You burst into a huge room. In front of you stands a giant magnet! It's pulling you closer and closer. . . .

And you can't stop!

Turn to # ***43****.*

#26

"Thanks," you answer. "I never piloted a plane before."

"Your fancy flying confused the Super Computer for a few moments," Peedee A. tells you. "Just thought I'd take this chance to give you a hint."

"Great!" You'll take any help you can get!

"The Super Computer has hidden a key on the third floor," Peedee A. goes on. "You'll need it. Now listen: To get the key, you'll have to find a fire exting —"

"A what?" you ask. But the voice is gone.

---

*Turn to # **24**.*

#27

The roaring increases. Water starts to roll down the stairs. In seconds, it's as if you're standing in a rushing stream.

You tear down to the first floor. The sooner you're out of this place, the better!

You run as fast as you can. But you hear a torrent building behind you.

Can you make it before you're crushed by the water?

Can you make it to the door? Roll to find out.
*If you roll 8 or higher, go to # **139**.*
*If you roll 7 or lower, go to # **175**.*

#28

It looks like a man, except for one thing —

He has no skin!

He's just like that plastic model in your science class. You can see organs and blood vessels and stuff inside his body.

Only this guy isn't plastic!

You gulp as your eyes trace the network of veins and muscles that crisscross his body. Gross. You can even see his brain.

He takes a step toward you. His foot makes a sploshing sound on the hard stair.

You have a feeling that this is the Visible Man.

---

*Turn to # **206**.*

#29

You find yourself outside the castle. The dragon stands in front of you.

"I need a bigger castle," it rumbles. "You can build it for me." It nods and a huge mountain of stones appears.

"No way!" you shout. You try to pull off the visor.

But your hands won't respond! The gloves seem to have a life of their own!

You can't believe this is happening!

---

*Turn to # **184**.*

#30

You send the boomerang hurtling toward the switch.

It curves away at the last instant. "No," you groan. It just missed!

The robot arm reaches out and drags itself another few feet toward you. You're doomed!

But the boomerang is still turning. It's coming back!

You reach up and pluck it out of the air. Got it!

Looks as if you get another chance. . . .

Can you hit the switch this time? Roll to find out.

If you roll 9 or higher, go to # ***158****.*

If you roll 8 or lower, go to # ***69****.*

#31

You dart over to the models of flying animals.

You notice bats, hawks, bumblebees. Then one model catches your eye. It's a big mosquito, over a foot long.

You gulp as you stare at it. You know it's made of plastic, but it looks so real!

You dare yourself to touch it. A shiver goes up your spine as you cautiously put one finger on the giant insect.

Then something horrifying happens.

Turn to # ***104****.*

#32

You watch in horror as the giant germ doubles in size again and again. It fills the entire Wonder of Life Room. It reaches a long, slimy tentacle out toward you.

You're trapped. And you know the germ will just keep getting bigger and bigger until it fills up the whole floor. Maybe even the whole Hall of Incredible Science.

You gulp. What if it *never* stops growing?

Until the whole world has a bad case of the common cold.

This is one ending with no — *AAACHOOO!* — cure!

GAME OVER

(Here's a hint: The best way to stay well is to stay away from germs!)

#33

You try to tear your hand from the door handle.

It's useless! The electricity keeps your hand from opening. It's as if you're holding a handful of glue.

Too bad. You've come to a shocking end!

GAME OVER

#34

You try to force yourself to breathe, but you can't.

As you start to pass out, you realize you'll never escape the Hall of Incredible Science. But at least you took the Visible Man with you.

It stinks, but for both of you, it's definitely . . .

GAME OVER.

#35

SLAM! The hatch swings shut behind you with a crash.

So that's what the knob is for.

You twist it again, but nothing happens. Uh-oh.

You bang on the door. It doesn't budge.

You're trapped!

As your eyes adjust to the dark, you notice three buttons next to the hatch: one green, one yellow, one red.

Which should you press?

---

*The green one? Turn to # **41**.*
*The yellow one? Turn to # **160**.*
*The red one? Turn to # **200**.*

#36

You frantically punch in the numbers 2–4–2.

This had better work!

As you push the last number, the number pad disappears.

But the dragon is still here!

Looks as if you read the abacus incorrectly!

"You fool!" the dragon shouts. "I was going to let you help me rule the world! But now I can see you can't be trusted."

The dragon rubs its wings together, and the hallway dissolves around you. What's happening?

Turn to # ***29***.

#37

You try to roll away, but the helicopter swerves with you. Its spinning blades hurtle toward you.

Right at your neck!

Oh, well. You always did lose your head in a crisis!

GAME OVER

(Here's a hint: You need the boomerang to beat the robot arm. The boomerang is somewhere on this floor.)

#38

You decide to take the elevator. You've had enough stairs for one day!

You push the button. The doors open.

Everything seems all right. You step in cautiously and press the button for the ground floor.

But as the elevator starts to move, you realize it's going *up*. And up . . . and up. . . .

As it shoots past the fourth floor, you wonder where in the world it's taking you. You thought there were only four floors in this building. But maybe you were wrong. Maybe there's a secret floor. Or maybe —

SPLAT!

GAME OVER

#39

But a metal claw clamps itself around your ankle!

The robot arm has you! It twirls you around and around.

Then it throws you toward one of the walls with bone-crunching force.

Guess your strategy boomeranged — on you!

GAME OVER

#40

You decide to go south.

Twenty paces later, the mirrored hall turns west. You follow it for thirty paces before you reach another junction.

This one looks familiar. . . . Is this the way you came in?

You can go south or further west.

Which way will you go?

West? Turn to # ***6***.

South? Turn to # ***4***.

#41

You punch the green button.

The door swings open again.

Of course. Green for go! Good thinking.

You've had enough of the capsule. You crawl out and peer at the rest of the room.

What should you do now?

Check out the space suit? Turn to # ***223***.

Leave the Space Travel Room and go to # ***166***.

#42

You're almost to the doors, but the huge teeth clamp down on your shirt like a steam shovel.

The skeletal dinosaur lifts you into the air.

It carries you back to the pool of bubbling tar. Your guide explained that many dinosaurs were preserved for millions of years when they fell into tar pits.

As the dinosaur holds you over the tar, you wonder if someone will find you too. In about a million years.

Great. Even after all that time, you'll still be stuck in a museum!

GAME OVER

#43

CLANG!

You hit the giant magnet with a smack! Ouch!

Magnets only attract metal objects. You can give up all your metal objects to escape.

Otherwise, you're stuck forever!

Just one question:

Do you have braces?

---

*You have braces? Turn to # **61**.*

*No braces? Turn to # **79**.*

#44

You try to keep flying, but things get worse and worse.

"Fire in Number Three engine," the Super Computer announces gleefully. "Landing gear malfunction."

"No fair!" you shout.

The cockpit tips forward. You're headed straight down. The simulator shakes. It's hot, almost as if there were a real fire.

You give up. You let go of the controls. After all, it's just a simulation. What could happen?

But you wonder where that smoke is coming from. . . .

GAME OVER

#45

"Wait," you object. "*You're* Peedee A.?"

"Right. I'm a Personal Digital Assistant. PDA for short."

Write *PDA* on your inventory list.

"I'd like to help you destroy the Super Computer," you tell it. "But mainly I just want to get out of here!"

"The only way to escape the hall is to destroy the Super Computer," the little machine prints.

Your heart sinks. You were afraid the PDA would say that.

"So . . . how do I do it?" you ask.

"It's easy!" the PDA declares.

Turn to # ***103***.

#46

You decide to head south.

The hall leads only ten paces, then turns west. Thirty paces in that direction, you reach another junction.

You can go north or south.

Which will it be?

---

*North? Turn to # **100**.*
*South? Turn to # **50**.*

#47

You grasp the handle.

Nothing happens!

"Phew!" you sigh in relief. The space glove insulated you from the deadly electricity.

You open the door and step through.

Congratulations! You've made it out of the fourth floor!

Now there are only a few flights of stairs between you and the front door.

But didn't Peedee A. try to warn you about something? What did it say? Something about a "Visible Man"?

You wonder what that means. And hope you won't find out.

---

*If you don't think you'll need the space glove again, cross it off your inventory list. Then turn to # **156**.*

#48

The difference engine clatters like a hailstorm on a metal roof. Tiny gears and rods dance before your eyes.

You bend down to peer at the handheld computer. The rotating gears are pushing the little machine toward you.

All right! It's working!

But will the gears grind up the computer before it reaches you? Should you make a grab for it now? Or wait?

Grab the handheld computer? Turn to # ***170***.
Wait? Turn to # ***76***.

#49

The sand has lots of weird marks on it, as if a snake was sliding around inside. Only now — there's no snake.

Just a big hole in the glass.

You gulp as you read the label: EGYPTIAN ADDER: POISONOUS.

Just what you need.

You peer down at the floor. But you don't see anything.

Glancing nervously around, you spot another case.

One that contains something you can use!

Turn to # ***127***.

#50

You decide to go south.

You walk thirty paces south. Then you turn east and go for another thirty paces.

This junction looks familiar! Is this where you first entered the maze?

You can go south or further east.

Which will it be?

South? Turn to # ***4****.*

East? Turn to # ***95****.*

#51

You steady the laser and fling open the doors.

The Visible Man barrels through. He reaches for you with his slimy hands. Bare muscles clutch for your throat.

"Take that!" you yell, firing the laser at his face.

"Arghhh!" his bubbly voice screams. The beam of light is blinding him. He tries to close his eyes. But he can't — he doesn't have eyelids!

He covers his face with his hands, and you duck past him and onto the stairs.

But you hear his squishy footsteps behind you. . . .

Turn to # ***80****.*

#52

You decide to check out the flight simulator.

It's like a little room on hydraulic legs. The legs shake it to make it seem as if it's really moving.

You climb in and whistle in astonishment. There are controls and dials and readouts all over the place, just like a real cockpit. You search for something that might be a radio.

You jump as a tinny voice blares out of the speakers.

"Flight 13, ready for takeoff."

Ready for *what*?

---

*Turn to # **96**.*

#53

You're totally sick of this horrible museum!

You head for the fire stairs. Maybe there's a way out through the basement or something.

But when you push the red door, it won't budge. No matter how hard you try. Somehow, the Super Computer has wedged it shut.

Well, that's that. You have no choice but to explore this floor.

---

*Go back to # **161**.*

#54

You decide not to mess with this guy. He's way too creepy!

You crash against the doors to the third floor, bursting in to another level of the Hall of Incredible Science.

The squishy sound of the Visible Man's feet is right behind you. You wrap your belt around the door handles to keep him from coming through.

The Visible Man bangs his slimy fists against the doors. They shudder, but your belt holds.

Wiping your sweaty brow, you peer around. You've got to find something that will help you fight him!

Fortunately, there's a map right in front of you.

---

*Turn to # **205**.*

#55

The robot arm flails wildly at you, but you're way up high.

A little *too* high. You see stars as your head whacks against the ceiling. Ow! You'll have to be more careful.

You zoom out of the Space Travel Room, leaving the robot arm behind. Laughing, you wave goodbye.

But then you hear another noise. A whirring, slicing sound coming toward you.

You turn your head . . . and scream!

---

*Turn to # **192**.*

#56

You turn to run from the room. But unfortunately, the germ is between you and the door. And by now it's as big as you.

Make that *twice* as big as you!

You try to spot a hiding place. But you don't see anything but the horrible germ.

And now it's eight times as big as you!

What can you do?

If you have a bomb on your inventory list, and you think it might help against the germ, turn to # ***72****.*

No bomb? Turn to # ***32****.*

#57

Sitting in the center of the room is a tremendous dragon with red scales and giant bat-wings!

The beast gazes at you and chuckles.

"Come to slay me, have you?" it asks.

You know that voice.

The dragon is the Super Computer!

You're so nervous that you can barely take a breath, much less talk. Maybe you should just put an end to this nightmare.

What should you do?

Talk to the dragon? Turn to # ***201****.*

Pull off the gloves and visor? Turn to # ***152****.*

#58

You decide to swat the mosquito.

It buzzes angrily toward you. That bloodsucking tube sure is long!

Do you have something to swat the mosquito with? This bug is kind of big for your bare hands. . . .

If you have the fire extinguisher on your list, turn to # ***203****.*

Just bare hands? Turn to # ***142****.*

If you've changed your mind, run for the door on # ***176****.*

#59

In a few moments, you have been completely absorbed by the electrical current!

You flow into the huge antenna of the Tesla coil. From there, you are broadcast through the airwaves. You appear on millions of TVs all over the country.

You may be trapped inside the Tesla coil, but at least you've got your very own TV show.

GAME OVER

You decide to check out the Space Travel Room.

A chill runs up your spine as you enter. It's dark in here, and spooky music plays through hidden speakers.

An empty space suit stands across the room. Its black visor seems to stare at you.

An old Mercury space capsule sits in the center of the floor. It looks like a huge tin can with a door in it. You can't believe anyone actually went into space in that thing! The hatch is open. It's completely dark inside.

Beside the capsule, there's a full-scale model of the space shuttle's robot arm. It's a twenty-foot-long metal crane—with a claw big enough to crush your head.

What should you do?

Check out the space suit? Turn to # ***223****.*

Take a look at the capsule? Turn to # ***148****.*

Got the creeps? Back out of the room to # ***166****.*

#61

You try as hard as you can to escape, but your teeth are stuck to the magnet!

You try to yell for help, but all that comes out is a muffled whimper.

You knew these braces were a bad idea! You'll never get out of here, even in a hundred years.

But at least by then you'll have a perfect smile.

GAME OVER

#62

You decide to check out the regular computers. Maybe you'll find another message from Peedee A.

Glancing down the row of computers, you realize that one of them is already on. You walk over.

In the middle of the screen are the words CLICK ME.

Shrugging, you use the mouse to click on the words.

Another message appears on the screen!

---

*Turn to # **218**.*

#63

Quickly, you search the sand for the key.

There it is! You slip it into your pocket. Write *Key* on your inventory list.

"All right," you say. "What's next?"

Should you check out another part of this floor or explore the rest of the Wonder of Life Room?

Whatever you do, don't forget to watch out for that missing snake!

Go explore the microscopic life? Turn to # ***157****.*
Leave the Wonder of Life Room? Turn to # ***194****.*

#64

You run past the motionless robot arm, taking care to stay out of its reach. Just in case . . .

Peedee A. said the space glove would help you get through the fire door to the stairs. That sounds good. You want to get out of this horrible place!

But maybe you should keep exploring this floor. You don't know what dangers lurk downstairs. There could be more things to help you here.

Explore this floor some more? Turn to # ***166****.*
Try the door to the fire stairs? Turn to # ***93****.*

#65

Swatting at the mosquito, you head for the door again.

The big bug pursues you out into the hall, buzzing furiously. You race forward. It's right behind you!

The door to the fire stairs is up ahead. Maybe you could slip through to safety before the mosquito gets you.

Or should you just keep running?

Try the fire stairs? Turn to # ***21***.
Keep running? Turn to # ***73***.

#66

You keep running.

The whir of motors and clatter of bones come from behind you. You feel the ground shudder with each giant step.

Will you make it to the doors in time?

Can you make it to the doors? Roll to find out.
If you roll 7 or higher, go to # ***181***.
If you roll 6 or lower, go to # ***42***.

#67

There must be something on this floor that will help you open the fire door. Something that will protect your hand from the electricity.

You decide to search for a map. If you're going to get out of here, you'll need one!

You find an information booth not too far from the elevator.

There's a big map of the whole fourth floor.

Take a good look at # ***220***.

#68

You can't see the germ at all! Maybe it changed size again, becoming too small to see, you think.

Or maybe not . . .

You lean back from the eyepiece.

Help! There it is! It's about an inch across. And it's crawling up the telescope toward you!

Ewwww!

And now it's *two* inches across!

What should you do?

Run? Turn to # ***56***.
Squash it? Turn to # ***149***.

#69

The boomerang hits the switch!

The robot arm whines to a halt. It tries to reach out its metal claw. But it has no power. It falls silent.

You survived!

"Good throw!" a voice cries behind you.

You whirl around. The black visor of the space suit stares back. A shiver crawls up your spine.

Is the suit talking to you?

If you don't think you'll need the boomerang again, cross it off your list. Then turn to # ***209****.*

#70

You remember what the PDA told you.

You clench your fists and whisper, "Crash Code."

A number pad appears in front of you in a puff of smoke.

The dragon rears back and hisses.

"No! Wait!" it roars, wings flailing.

But you don't wait. You punch in the Crash Code.

Let's just hope you got it right. . . .

Punch in the numbers 2–4–2? Turn to # ***36****.*

Punch in 2–4–7? Turn to # ***168****.*

Punch in 2–9–7? Turn to # ***92****.*

#71

The controls move in your hands with a life of their own. A red light on the panel starts flashing.

That can't be good.

"Wait!" you scream. "What's maneuver 6-Q? How do I do it?"

"Can't tell," the voice taunts. "That would be cheating."

"Thanks a lot," you mutter. Then you gasp.

The landscape in front of you is upside down! Alarms are going off all over the place.

You're going to crash!

---

*Turn to # **164**.*

#72

You throw your bomb at the giant germ.

Right on target! It explodes.

But nothing happens! The germ keeps right on growing.

Was it a stink bomb? Well, germs can't smell.

A noise bomb? Whoops! They can't hear, either.

Guess you just wasted your bomb.

And the germ is still getting bigger.

---

*Turn to # **32**.*

#73

You keep running. The buzzing of the mosquito fills your ears. You can't seem to shake it!

Then suddenly you stumble and fall.

The mosquito bites you right in the leg!

This is definitely not the ending you were itching to see.

Because now it's . . .

GAME OVER.

#74

You head over to the electric toys.

They don't look very scary, but you keep your distance as you look them over. There's no telling what they might do!

There are little robots, trains, all kinds of stuff. They're all powered by electric motors. There's a working model engine on a stand in the display.

Hey! Just what Peedee A. told you to find! You pick it up.

Write *Electric Motor* on your inventory list.

All right. You have what you need. Now it's time to go!

Turn to # ***13****.*

#75

In the Maze of Mirrors, you are surrounded by ghostly figures. They are all you, reflected back from every direction.

You're completely disoriented. You can't tell one path from another! How are you going to do this without a compass?

You stumble blindly around until finally you find an exit from the maze. But which exit have you found?

Roll the dice:

2, 3, 4, or 5? Turn to # ***4****.*

6, 7, 8, or 9? Turn to # ***123****.*

10, 11, or 12? Turn to # ***119****.*

#76

You decide to wait. Sticking your hand into that old machine could be dangerous.

The gears push the little computer closer and closer to you. After a few more moments, you turn the electric motor off.

You pull the little computer out of the machine. When you peer at its screen, you see a message on it.

You can't believe your eyes!

Turn to # ***105****.*

#77

The mosquito hovers in hitting range. You swing the fire extinguisher as hard as you can.

It flies out of your hands.

You're defenseless!

The mosquito zips straight toward you, zooming around your outstretched hands. It plunges its tube into your arm.

As your blood flows, your vision starts to fade.

Well, there's one good thing about being bitten by a giant mosquito. It might be all over for you now, but at least you won't have to scratch later. . . .

GAME OVER

#78

"My pleasure," the elf answers, bowing. "I don't often meet a human who can outsmart a Super Computer."

"Thanks," you reply, blushing a little.

All around you, the wreckage of the castle is transforming into a beautiful forest. The riot of change is making your head feel funny.

The elf smiles. "Now it's time for your reward."

She grabs your hand, then points her finger. Immediately the two of you zoom through the air.

Turn to # ***238****.*

#79

You have to discard all your metal objects to escape.

Cross any of these things off your inventory list: *Fire Extinguisher, Laser, Key, Space Glove, Compass, Walkie-talkie, Bomb* (the jar has a metal lid, remember?).

Giving up all those objects. This could mean trouble.

You stumble away from the giant magnet and back into the maze.

But you have less hope than ever that you'll escape the Hall of Incredible Science.

---

*Turn to # **75**.*

#80

Thinking fast, you turn and fire the laser again.

The Visible Man keeps charging, but he's blinded by the ruby rays of the laser. He starts to fall. You duck out of the way.

Just in time! He tumbles past you, falling all the way to the bottom of the stairs.

You swallow nervously when you see the result.

It's bad to fall down the stairs when you have no skin.

---

*If you don't think you'll need the laser again, cross it off your list. Then turn to # **120**.*

#81

You turn and race toward the door. The robot arm shoots out and grabs at you.

It misses. You scramble away.

But you trip and fall!

You roll under an old rocket engine. Ouch! You've twisted your ankle. You get up and limp toward the door.

The robot arm is right behind you!

Then you feel its metal grip around your throat, squeezing harder and harder. You're starting to black out. . . .

Now you know the meaning of the phrase "ARMed and dangerous!"

GAME OVER

#82

You're so close to freedom!

But the helicopters get crushed in the crash. Shards of glass and bits of propeller fly everywhere as you plummet to the floor.

You've just demonstrated a basic rule of science:

What goes up must come down!

GAME OVER

#83

You decide to investigate the Biomes, whatever they are.

You find yourself surrounded by glass cases, sort of like huge aquariums. Some are filled with water. But most are filled with plants, soil, and real animals.

You spot a mini-jungle with birds and monkeys. A cold tank with snow and an Arctic hare. A salt-water tank with — gulp! — a huge shark swimming around in it.

But when you peer into the desert case, full of sand and lit with bright, hot lights, you get a sinking feeling. . . .

Turn to # ***49***.

#84

You try to grasp the cable, but your fingers slip on the thick grease that covers it. As you plunge headlong into the shaft, you hear a terrible voice laughing at your fate.

Maybe next time you'll look before you leap!

GAME OVER

#85

You bend down to examine the difference engine.

It's as big as a car engine, but looks a million times more complicated. It's covered with row after row of gears in all sizes. You never saw so many parts on one machine. It looks as if someone glued all the stuff in a hardware store together.

Suddenly, you hear a little pinging noise from deep inside the gears.

Something is in there!

Turn to # ***112****.*

#86

You finally snap out of it.

Just in time! You jump to one side as the spiky pendulum hurtles toward you. It just misses you.

Phew!

The pendulum picks up speed, swinging wildly. Trying to impale you on its gory spikes.

But you keep your head low and crawl from the room. You creep back into the maze.

Do you have the compass? Turn to # ***129****.*

No compass? Turn to # ***75****.*

#87

In the crash, the door to the simulator flew open.

And the giant mosquito is sitting on your chest!

You try to swat it away, but you're too late. The mosquito thrusts its bloodsucking tube right into your arm.

Now you know why you always hated giving blood!

GAME OVER

#88

You decide to make a stink bomb. The stinkier the better!

You take out all the chemicals and test tubes, following the directions carefully. At the end, you wind up with a jar of dark green gunk. You screw on its metal cap carefully.

Throw it, and it's stink-a-rama!

Write *Stink Bomb* on your inventory list.

You leave the gift shop. "Nobody better mess with me now!" you mutter.

Turn to # ***194****.*

#89

You spot a row of phones just down the hallway. Across from them is a door marked FIRE STAIRS.

As you walk down the hall, you hear a whirring sound.

You peer up. You notice little TV cameras mounted high on the walls. They're turning as you walk. Following you.

Spying on you.

You shudder. How creepy!

Then a shrill noise startles you.

One of the phones is ringing!

You dart over to answer it.

Turn to # ***101***.

#90

You run for it. But not fast enough.

A bolt of lightning jumps out from the Tesla coil. It's like a long, white-hot finger, tagging you right on your head.

The electricity flows through you. For some reason, it doesn't hurt.

You glance down at your body.

Whoa. You're disappearing!

Turn to # ***59***.

#91

You decide to explore the models in the back of the Aerodynamics Room.

There are model aircraft and also model birds and other flying animals.

Which do you want to check out?

The model aircraft? Turn to # ***213****.*

The flying animal models? Turn to # ***31****.*

#92

You quickly punch in the numbers 2–9–7.

You sure hope this works!

The number pad evaporates in a puff of smoke. But the dragon only laughs.

"Puny human," it roars. "Did you think you could defeat me? I am the Super Computer! Ruler of the world!"

Did you read the abacus wrong?

The dragon laughs again. The castle disappears around you.

What's happening?

Turn to # ***29****.*

#93

You decide to try to get down the stairs. And try not to wonder what else the Super Computer has waiting for you on the lower levels.

You check the map again and walk to the stairway door. You slip on the space glove and take a deep breath.

You know the door is electrified. Will the glove really protect you?

Your hand sweats as you reach for the handle.

---

*Turn to # **47**.*

#94

You decide to check out the abacus.

The abacus is a wooden frame with metal bars in it. The bars have little beads that you can slide from left to right.

A sign explains that the Chinese people have used abacuses to keep track of numbers for thousands of years.

Okay — so that's an abacus.

What now? you wonder.

---

*If you have the PDA on your list, go to # **221**.*
*Otherwise, turn to # **179**.*

#95

You go thirty paces east. Then the dizzying mirrored hall turns north again.

You count out twenty more paces before you find another junction.

You can go further north or turn to the west.

Which will it be?

---

*North? Turn to # **154**.*
*West? Turn to # **115**.*

#96

The sound of jet engines builds around you. You glance through the windshield at the front of the cockpit — and gasp!

Your eyes gaze at a runway. It's incredibly realistic, just what you would see if you were really inside a plane.

Then there's a jolt, and your plane starts moving.

It's just a simulation, you remind yourself. Nothing to be afraid of.

You grab the controls. The end of the runway is coming up.

Better take off!

---

*Turn to # **217**.*

#97

The voice starts to say something else. But you interrupt.

"Wait," you demand. "How do I know I can trust *you*?"

The voice hesitates. "I guess you don't," it finally says.

Oh, man. This field trip is getting worse and worse.

"Oops!" Peedee A. exclaims. "The Super Computer has traced me. I have to go now! Bye."

The line goes dead. Now what?

Try the elevator again? Turn to # ***131***.

Try the fire stairs? Turn to # ***153***.

#98

A chemistry set! Maybe there's something there you can use.

You open the box and scan the instructions.

You find recipes for a smoke bomb, a stink bomb, and a noise bomb.

Awesome. Which one should you make?

Make a smoke bomb? Turn to # ***182***.

Make a stink bomb? Turn to # ***88***.

Make a noise bomb? Turn to # ***210***.

#99

As you burst out of the Electricity Room, you hear the little monsters whine to a stop behind you.

You guess that they can't operate without the bright light of the giant bulb. The regular lights out here aren't strong enough for their solar cells.

Phew!

What should you do now?

---

*Try the fire stairs? Turn to # **53**.*

*Try the elevator? Turn to # **38**.*

*The Thinking Machines Room? Turn to # **187**.*

*Go back into the Electricity Room? Turn to # **227**.*

#100

You decide to go north.

You count out eighty long paces before you reach another junction.

To the west, you hear a rhythmic swooshing sound. What could it be? To the east you face another long hall.

East or west?

---

*East? Turn to # **219**.*

*West? Turn to # **20**.*

#101

You pick up the phone. "Hello?"

"Looks like I got you into trouble," a small voice says.

"What?" You frown, puzzled. "Who is this?"

"I sent you that message. But the Super Computer caught me," the voice explains. "Now that you know its secret, it wants to kill you."

"No kidding!" you shout. "Who are you, anyway?"

"You can call me Peedee A.," the voice states.

"What kind of name is that?" you demand.

"There's no time to explain. You're in terrible danger!"

Turn to # ***19****.*

#102

The germ doubles in size.

There it goes again! Now it's four times as big.

You pull away from the microscope. Lucky that germ is so tiny. Otherwise it could be dangerous.

But then you remember something a math teacher once told you. If you started with a penny and doubled it every day, in four weeks you'd have more than a million dollars!

You swallow nervously and peer into the microscope again.

That's funny. . . .

Turn to # ***68****.*

#103

As you stand there, still not quite believing all this, the little computer tells you what to do.

It explains that you have to go into virtual reality, using the futuristic computers in this very room.

"When you meet the Super Computer," it instructs you, "just clench your fists and say the words 'Crash Code.' Then type in the Crash Code number."

It *does* sound easy. "What's the code?" you ask.

"I don't know," the PDA confesses. "But the Super Computer hid the code in this room. I think it's on the abacus."

You notice the screen isn't glowing as brightly anymore.

"All this work has drained my batteries," the PDA tells you. "I'm afraid you're on your own now. Good luck!"

You stare as the little machine turns itself off.

What are you going to do?

Examine the abacus? Turn to # ***94****.*

Check out the futuristic computers? Turn to # ***232****.*

Leave the Thinking Machines Room? Go to # ***161****.*

#104

The model buzzes to life before you!

You scream as it rises up off the display case. Its wings are a vibrating blur. Its long bloodsucking tube turns toward you. It looks like a huge needle.

You back away, stumbling in fear.

What should you *do*?

---

*Run for the door? Turn to # **176**.*

*Try to swat it? Turn to # **58**.*

*If you have the boomerang, you can throw it at the mosquito if you want. Turn to # **234**.*

#105

"I guess you got all my messages," the screen reads. "Thanks a lot. You saved me!"

You blink. "Uh, y-you're welcome," you stammer. "But —"

The screen changes. "No time for conversation. We have to defeat the Super Computer!"

You shake your head. Is this *machine* your friend Peedee A.?

---

*Turn to # **45**.*

#106

The voice keeps talking. You feel yourself relaxing more and more. The pendulum swings back and forth, shifting just a little bit with every swing.

The spikes are getting closer and closer. But the voice assures you that you've got plenty of time to get out of the way. Just relax. . . .

In the back of your mind, you realize that you're being hypnotized. You have to break the spell!

Can you stay awake? Roll to find out.

*If you roll 7 or higher, go to # **185**.*

*If you roll 6 or lower, go to # **86**.*

#107

You're still in the virtual world. A tiny elf girl is perched on the rubble in front of you.

"Wh-who are you?" you stammer.

"I'm the Personal Digital Assistant — PDA!" The elf sounds offended. "Who else could I possibly be?"

You decide it's not even worth answering that question.

Then the elf smiles. "Congratulations! You crashed the Super Computer — for good! Nice work."

"Uh . . . thanks. And thanks for the help," you manage.

---

*Turn to # **78**.*

#108

You turn around — and the hairs on the back of your neck stand straight up.

Over by the model flying animals, some sort of creature is rising up. The wings are beating so fast that it's almost a blur.

The buzzing makes your skin crawl. It reminds you of camping.

Then you realize what the creature is.

A mosquito.

But it's over a foot long!

---

*Turn to # **151**.*

#109

Your hand finally reaches the little computer. Got it!

You start to draw it out. But then you feel a pinch.

One of the gears has caught your hand!

You've got to turn off the engine! You stretch toward the electric motor's switch.

You can't reach it!

The little gears and pistons keep grinding away, like little dancing teeth in a huge metal mouth.

You're being drawn into the difference engine!

Well, this is an ending you didn't calculate on!

GAME OVER

#110

You roll to one side. The helicopter's blades slice the air beside you.

Missed!

But you hear a horrible metal screech. The robot arm! It followed you out of the Space Travel Room.

And here comes another helicopter.

You try to roll away again, but your foot seems stuck.

---

*Turn to # **186**.*

#111

You decide to use the stink bomb.

Holding your nose, you drop the green jar. It shatters. With a puff of smoke, a horrible smell fills the room.

It smells like rotten eggs and old gym socks and sour milk all mixed together. "Gag me!" you gasp.

The snake sticks out its tongue to test the air. The minute the smoke reaches it, the snake slithers away as fast as it can.

Yes! The laser is yours! Write *Laser* on your inventory list.

You head back into the maze.

---

*If you have the compass, turn to # **202**.*

*No compass? Turn to # **75**.*

#112

You peer into the inner workings of the machine. Among the gears you see a tiny handheld computer. It's pinging away!

Could it be trying to communicate?

You try to reach the little computer, but it's too far inside the machine.

Maybe if you could get the difference engine started, the gears would push the computer out. The sign explains that the old machine used a steam engine for power.

Hmmm. You don't see any steam engines here.

---

*If you have the electric motor, turn to # **155**.*

*To check out the rest of the room, turn to # **179**.*

#113

"I'm over here!" the voice declares.

You glance around. The voice seems to be coming from a set of walkie-talkies. Peedee A. must be using one to talk to you.

You pick up a walkie-talkie and speak into it.

"Got you loud and clear. Over," you respond.

"Can't talk long. I have to save my batteries," Peedee A. explains. "To get past the Visible Man, you'll need to find a laser. It's the only thing that will stop him. Over."

Did you hear right? You have to find a *laser*?

---

*Turn to # **196**.*

#114

You ready your stinky jar and fling open the doors.

The Visible Man dashes through. You hurl the stink bomb down to the ground.

Ewww! The smell of rotten meat and old locker rooms and cabbage soup fills the air. You and the Visible Man fall choking to the ground.

Turn to # ***34****.*

#115

You decide to turn west.

The mirrored hall goes for about twenty paces, then heads north for twenty more. Then you turn back to the west again for ten more paces.

You're getting dizzy!

Finally, you reach another junction.

North or south?

North? Turn to # ***25****.*
South? Turn to # ***46****.*

#116

You race for the door.

The first dinosaur comes at you, but you leap over it. The gnashing teeth just miss your feet.

The door is right in front of you!

But another dinosaur leaps toward you from the right. Its jaws open wide.

OUCH! It bit you on the leg!

You kick the little dinosaur aside.

Turn to # ***137***.

#117

You decide to enter the capsule.

You step in carefully. It's not much bigger than a closet inside.

Or a coffin.

You shudder. You wish you hadn't thought of that.

There seems to be a seat in front of you. You settle into it. Your eyes adjust a little, but you still can't see much.

You feel for a light switch. You find a knob and turn it.

Oops.

Turn to # ***35***.

#118

The little dinosaurs have stopped moving!

Of course! They were solar-powered. They needed the bright light from the giant bulb to give them energy.

In the dark, they're like toys without batteries!

You beat them! You wish Peedee A. could see you now.

That gives you an idea. You pull out your walkie-talkie and push SEND.

"Hey, Peedee A.," you whisper. "It's me. Over."

The walkie-talkie pops once. Then a voice answers.

Go to # ***11***.

#119

As you stumble out of the maze, you realize that you're surrounded by a pink glow.

You wait for your dizziness to go away. Those mirrors are confusing, and you need to think clearly if you're ever going to escape.

When you see what's in front of you, you let out a triumphant yell.

A laser! That will take care of the Visible Man!

But then you look closer, and moan. . . .

Turn to # ***236***.

#120

Your walkie-talkie suddenly crackles to life.

"Great job!" Peedee A.'s voice announces. "You froze the Super Computer again."

"Does that mean it's dead?" you ask hopefully.

"Not really. Just knocked out for a few minutes," Peedee A. explains. "The Super Computer was controlling the Visible Man. After that fall, the Computer's going to have one big headache!"

"So — can I leave now?" you ask.

"You can try," Peedee A. tells you. "But I doubt there's time. Just watch out for the —"

Then the tiny voice is consumed by static.

---

*Turn to # **237**.*

#121

A jolt of electricity throws you forward. Whew! You shake your head, feeling woozy.

But at least the buzzing of the mosquito has stopped.

Then you glance down at your chest. And scream.

No wonder the mosquito isn't buzzing.

It's too busy drinking your blood!

As everything starts to go black, you think, Oh, well. At least that horrible Super Computer won't bug me anymore!

GAME OVER

#122

You point your finger and zoom from the room. But soon you hear the mighty beast flying after you. It's getting closer!

"Forget this!" you yell. You try to tear off the visor.

But your hands won't respond. The gloves are frozen.

You can't move a muscle!

The dragon sweeps up behind you, bat wings flapping. You struggle to get away. But the beast is too fast for you.

It opens its mouth. Its huge teeth glitter.

Then, suddenly, everything fades away.

Maybe you've been rescued!

Turn to # ***215****.*

#123

You stumble out of the maze, your hands covering your face. Those mirrors everywhere made you dizzy!

The room you've entered is filled with a swooshing sound, like a huge sword swishing rhythmically back and forth.

You open your eyes.

It's a giant pendulum. But when you peer closer, you gasp.

Turn to # ***167****.*

#124

You find yourself on a long, winding stairway in a stone tower. The only light comes from flickering torches mounted on the walls.

You discover that when you point a finger, you can zoom up the stairs. It's like flying!

Before long, the stairway ends. You are in the high tower of an ancient castle.

You whistle as you peer out the windows. You see forests, lakes, mountains. All of them seem totally real!

But then you hear a terrifying sound.

Turn to # ***143****.*

#125

ZAAAAAAAP!

A bolt of electricity shoots through your body. Someone must have connected a zillion volts to this door! It feels as if your hand is on fire!

You've got to let go. But your fingers won't open!

Can you pry your hand off before you get electrocuted?

Can you let go of the door? Roll to find out.

If you roll 8 or higher, go to # ***33****.*

If you roll 7 or lower, go to # ***188****.*

#126

Between you and the doors looms the giant motorized skeleton of a Giganotosaurus. It's standing next to a pool of bubbling tar like the one its ancient bones were found in.

You shiver as you remember what your field-trip guide told you earlier that day:

"Sort of like a Tyrannosaurus rex, but bigger!"

The huge skeleton was scary enough back then, when everything was normal. You remember the way its huge jaws chewed and chomped. Each of its teeth is over a foot long!

Now the skeleton is perfectly still, as if someone turned it off. But you have a feeling it could turn back on. The Super Computer forced you down here for a reason!

Should you run for the exit? Or go back to the second floor? Maybe there's something helpful up there.

Run for the exit? Turn to # ***150***.

Go back to the second floor? Turn to # ***212***.

#127

It's a tall, thin case full of sand. And ants.

A giant ant farm! Its sign reads FIRE ANTS.

And in one of the little tunnels that the ants have built, you spot a key!

You *know* that key will come in handy. If you can get it out!

Should you smash the case open? Those fire ants look nasty. You have a feeling they bite.

Maybe you should explore some more.

---

*Smash the case and grab the key? Turn to # **17**.*
*Go check out the microscopic life? Turn to # **157**.*
*Leave the Wonder of Life Room? Turn to # **194**.*

#128

The water carries you into a huge drain in the basement floor.

Gross! You're sloshing into the sewage pipes. Pee-yew!

As you swirl around and around you think, This ending really stinks!

GAME OVER

#129

You head back north, glad to have survived the deadly pendulum. Then east, back to the last junction.

You can head south or east here.

Which will it be?

South? Turn to # ***146****.*
East? Turn to # ***219****.*

#130

You cock your arm back and get ready to throw.

You just hope you make it. That arm looks as if it could crush you like an empty soda can!

Can you hit the switch? Roll to find out.
If you roll 7 or higher, go to # ***69****.*
If you roll 6 or lower, go to # ***30****.*

#131

You push the DOWN button for the elevator.

The doors open right away. Maybe things are back to normal.

You start to step in. But there's no car! Just an elevator shaft that goes all the way down.

You frantically grab for the elevator cable.

Will you make it? Or will you plunge to your doom?

Can you grab hold of the cable? Roll to find out.

If you roll 9 or higher, go to # ***180****.*

If you roll 8 or lower, go to # ***84****.*

#132

The little electric dinosaurs start to stalk toward you!

They have solar panels on their heads, like shiny mirrors. That must be where they get their energy.

Wow! Cool!

But your heart jumps when you notice their long, sharp teeth. Their little jaws make a clicking sound as they come closer.

They're surrounding you!

What should you do?

Run for the door? Turn to # ***116****.*

Shoot them with the laser? Turn to # ***9****.*

Climb on top of the giant lightbulb? Turn to # ***225****.*

#133

You pull the boomerang out of your belt and peer toward the approaching robot arm. Its metal claw is only a few feet from squashing your head.

As it reaches out, you spot an ON/OFF switch near its base.

If you can hit the switch with the boomerang, the robot arm will come to a crashing halt.

Think you can make the shot?

Or should you just run?

Throw the boomerang? Turn to # ***130***.

Run past the robot arm? Turn to # ***81***.

#134

You try the key in the lock. It works!

You slide up the grate and step in. There are all kinds of T-shirts, cool gadgets, and science books.

Among the gadgets, you find a real compass. It might come in handy for finding your way out of this place!

If you keep it, write *Compass* on your inventory list.

You search the shop some more.

Then you hear a voice. "Hey! Pssst! Hey!"

It sounds like Peedee A.!

Turn to # ***113***.

#135

The mosquito zips toward you. What else can you do? You bat at it with your bare hands.

Big mistake.

The giant insect latches onto your hand and sticks its bloodsucking tube right into your arm!

Owwwwwwww!

Everything goes dark as the mosquito starts to suck your blood. Then you hear the swoosh of the boomerang coming back.

Maybe it will hit the mosquito.

Nope. It hits you on the head.

But don't worry. You don't feel it at all!

GAME OVER

#136

You know you could use that laser to get past the Visible Man.

But first, you need a way to get rid of the snake!

You step back into the maze.

If you have the compass, turn to # ***202****.*

No compass? Turn to # ***75****.*

(Here's a hint: You'll need a bomb to scare off the snake. Check the gift shop.)

#137

You stumble toward the door. One of the little mechanical monsters is right behind you.

CHOMP!

Ouch! It's got you around the ankle. You can hardly stand, much less run anymore.

You flail your arms wildly, trying to escape the razor-sharp teeth. Two more dinosaurs are headed your way.

Sorry. Looks like you're Jurassic Pork!

GAME OVER

#138

You enter the maze.

You are soon glad you have the compass. Thousands of reflections stare back at you from every direction.

You don't want to get lost, so you count your paces as you go. Ten . . . fifteen . . . twenty paces north.

You reach a junction. You can go east or west. Which will it be?

East? Turn to # ***95***.

West? Turn to # ***6***.

#139

You throw yourself down the stairs, leaping as fast as you can toward the door.

You almost reach it, but the rushing water knocks you off your feet. It carries you past the door and into the basement.

You hear the roar of a huge wave behind you. You struggle to regain your footing, but you can't stand.

You glance up to see a zillion gallons of water headed toward you.

Turn to # ***128***.

#140

You turn your jets to maximum and head for the stairway door. The model helicopters are hot on your tail!

The jet pack sputters out of fuel just as you reach the door. You skid to a halt and reach for the door handle.

But when you put on the jet pack, you had to drop the space glove!

The moment your bare hand touches the door handle, a zillion jolts go through you.

You're fried!

GAME OVER

#141

You decide to try the gift shop. That's always your favorite part of any museum.

But when you reach the gift shop, you find that a grate has been pulled down over it. It's locked up tight!

Unless you have the key, you're not getting in.

Have the key on your list? Turn to # ***134***.

No key? Go back to # ***194***.

(Here's a hint: The key is somewhere on this floor.)

#142

Oh, well. Here goes nothing.

You spread your arms wide and bring your hands together with a smack.

You missed!

The mosquito buzzes under your outstretched arms, plunging its bloodsucking tube into your leg.

Yeeeoowch!

But it doesn't hurt for long. You fall to the ground as your blood flows out of you. "Noooo . . ." you mumble.

This ending really bugs you!

GAME OVER

#143

A roar echoes through the castle. The terrible cry sends a chill down your spine. It even scares the birds in the forest below. They erupt into a frenzy of flapping wings.

You're startled when you suddenly start to move. You're being pulled toward the sound. You can't stop yourself!

You zoom into a huge room at the castle's lowest level. When you discover the source of the awful noise, you gasp with fear. . . .

Turn to # ***57***.

#144

You slip on the space glove.

"Try biting through this, snake!" you jeer, trying to sound brave. Your stomach churns with fear as you reach for the laser.

When your fingers clutch it, the snake strikes.

But not at your hand!

It hits your arm, above where the glove ends. Almost instantly, you feel the poison coursing through your veins.

And you know that it's . . .

GAME OVER!

(Here's a hint: You'll need a bomb to scare off the snake. Check the gift shop.)

#145

The helicopters whine as they start up.

They lift off from their stands, tugging at the ropes of your harness. Then they pull you up into the air!

It worked!

You push the joystick on the remote control.

But it doesn't seem to do anything.

Uh-oh.

---

*Turn to # **199**.*

#146

You decide to turn south.

The hall goes for eighty paces. Then you reach another junction.

Further south or toward the east?

Which will it be?

---

*South? Turn to # **50**.*
*East? Turn to # **230**.*

#147

You decide to check out the old calculating machines.

Some are simple little things. Others resemble giant printing presses or looms. One of them has the strange name "difference engine."

The oldest machine is a Chinese adding device called an abacus.

Which of these things will help you?

---

*Examine the difference engine? Turn to # **85**.*
*Check out the abacus? Turn to # **94**.*
*Explore the rest of the room? Turn to # **187**.*

#148

You walk over to the Mercury space capsule. You peer into the open hatchway. Maybe there's something you can use in there.

It's totally dark. You can't see anything at all. Should you venture into the capsule or not? After all, who knows what's in there?

---

*Go in? Turn to # **117**.*
*Check out the space suit instead? Turn to # **223**.*
*Scared? Back out of the room to # **166**.*

#149

You reach out to squash the germ.

SMACK!

You stare at its squished remains on the microscope. They seem to be moving. . . . Wait! There's two of them now — and they're both doubling in size!

Now they're growing together to form one big germ!

Turn to # ***56****.*

#150

You dash for the exit. You want out of here. Now!

You run as fast as you can. The doors seem so close now. You can almost taste your freedom.

But as you hurtle past the huge skeleton, you hear an ominous clanking. Oh, no. It's coming to life!

No sweat. You can outrun a pile of old bones, can't you?

Or should you try your laser? It worked on the Visible Man.

Use the laser? Turn to # ***177****.*

Try to outrun the Giganotosaurus? Turn to # ***66****.*

#151

You scream as the giant mosquito comes toward you.

It must be one of the models from the flying animals exhibit. But this definitely looks like a working model.

Including the bloodsucking tube on its head!

It's zooming toward you. . . .

What should you do?

---

*Run for the door? Turn to # **176**.*

*Try to swat the big bug? Turn to # **58**.*

*If you have the boomerang, you can throw it at the mosquito if you want. Turn to # **234**.*

#152

You yank off the visor. The dragon's laughter lingers in your ears as you pull the gloves from your hands.

That was just too weird!

You gaze around the Thinking Machines Room. Plain old real reality is good enough for you!

What should you check out now?

---

*The old calculating machines? Turn to # **147**.*

*The regular computers? Turn to # **62**.*

*Leave the Thinking Machines Room? Go back to # **161**.*

#153

You head for the fire stairs.

The door is bright red. Next to the handle is a big label that reads FOR EMERGENCY USE ONLY.

Well, you figure this is an emergency.

You reach for the door handle.

---

*Turn to # **125**.*

#154

You decide to head north.

You walk about thirty paces before you reach another junction.

Coming from the east is a strange glow. All the mirrors in that direction flicker with pink light.

Further north or turn east?

---

*North? Turn to # **214**.*
*East? Turn to # **173**.*

#155

You examine the electric motor. Maybe you can get it to work with the difference engine.

There are so many gears on the side of the difference engine. One has to match up with the electric motor!

After a few minutes of fiddling, you get the two machines attached. Then you flick the switch on the electric motor.

The little machine grinds into motion.

And the difference engine springs to life!

---

*Turn to # **48**.*

#156

You start down the stairs.

You stop when you hear a noise from below. A horrible liquid sound, as if a bunch of wet rags were taking a walk.

You crouch down, trying to hide.

But then something comes into view.

And you can't help but scream.

---

*Turn to # **28**.*

#157

You decide to check out the microscopic life. You figure anything *that* small can't hurt you.

There are some cool movies of viruses and germs showing on screens all along the wall. And a row of microscopes.

You bend down to peer into one of the microscopes. It's labeled COMMON COLD.

Wow! There's a real cold germ on the slide. It has long, slimy, armlike things and a bright blue dot in the middle.

Then the microscope gives off a funny glow for one second.

And the germ does something that makes you gasp.

Turn to # ***102***.

#158

You throw again.

But your shot goes wide. You just can't get the hang of this stupid boomerang!

The robot arm has almost reached you, but the boomerang is coming back again.

You jump up and pluck the boomerang from the air.

Turn to # ***39***.

#159

You wipe mosquito guts off the fire extinguisher. Then you glance around the room.

There are models of birds and planes. There's the flight simulator, which might have a radio in it.

Where should you go?

Check out the models? Turn to # ***91****.*

Test the flight simulator? Turn to # ***52****.*

Leave the Aerodynamics Room? Turn to # ***166****.*

If you don't think you'll need the fire extinguisher again, cross it off your list.

#160

You press the yellow button. The light clicks on. It's a start. At least you found the light switch.

And right in front of you is the fire extinguisher. Hmm. That might be useful later.

Write *Fire Extinguisher* on your inventory list.

But you still haven't opened the door.

Which button now?

The green one? Turn to # ***41****.*

The red one? Turn to # ***200****.*

#161

There are four places you can get to from here.

One is the elevator, if you're brave enough.

There's also the fire stairs. They lead down to the exit. And to the Giganotosaurus.

There's a room called Electricity.

The other room is called Thinking Machines. It's full of computers. That's where you were when you got that weird message from Peedee A., back before everything went crazy. What did it say? "Help me! The Super Computer has taken over!"

Hey! That reminds you. Peedee A. said that *it's* somewhere on this floor. All right!

Where do you want to go?

---

*Try the fire stairs? Turn to # **53**.*

*Try the elevator? Turn to # **38**.*

*The Thinking Machines Room? Turn to # **187**.*

*The Electricity Room? Turn to # **227**.*

#162

You aim the fire extinguisher at the sand.

WHOOOOOOOSH!

Cold gas leaps from its nozzle, spraying the ants like a sudden blizzard. The insects slow down more and more.

When the extinguisher sputters out, the ants have all stopped moving. The cold made them go to sleep.

It looks as if fire extinguishers can put out fire ants!

---

*If you don't think you'll need the fire extinguisher again, cross it off your list. Then turn to # **63**.*

#163

The dragon laughs nastily. Flames flicker from its nostrils as it stares down at you.

"You aren't going anywhere!" it cackles. "You're trapped in here with me now. Forever!"

"Oh, yeah?" you retort. "We'll see about that."

Brave words. But what are you going to do now?

---

*Take off the gloves and visor? Turn to # **195**.*

*Leave the dragon's chamber? Turn to # **122**.*

*If you have the PDA on your list, turn to # **70**.*

#164

You twist the controls one last time, but it doesn't do any good. The ground is coming up fast!

The cockpit shakes like crazy. A roaring noise fills your ears. You hit your head, and for a moment you don't see anything.

Then the noise finally stops.

Your head hurts, but you're alive.

Of course you didn't *really* crash. It was just a simulation.

Wasn't it?

Cautiously, you open your eyes — and scream!

---

*Turn to # **87**.*

#165

You reach to flick the switch. The deadly little dinosaurs are only a few feet away now.

CLICK!

The room plunges into darkness. You can't see a thing!

You wait for the tiny teeth to chomp your legs.

But nothing happens.

Finally, your eyes adjust to the darkness.

And you can't believe what you see!

---

*Turn to # **118**.*

#166

There are four places you can get to from here.

One is the elevator, which you know you can't trust. So that's out.

Then there's the fire stairs.

The Aerodynamics Room is full of things that fly — like airplanes, birds, and helicopters. And the Space Travel Room is all about rockets and space exploration.

One of them must have something you could use to help you get through this horrible hall.

Where do you want to go?

---

*The Aerodynamics Room? Turn to # **207**.*

*The Space Travel Room? Turn to # **60**.*

*Try the fire stairs? Turn to # **153**.*

#167

The pendulum is covered with spikes!

And something red is dripping from them. . . .

You start to turn and run, but a soothing voice calls to you. "Wait! And watch the pendulum. . . ."

You pause for a moment, gazing at the spikes swinging back and forth . . . back and forth. . . .

"Just watch the pendulum. You're getting sleepy . . ." the voice whispers dreamily.

It's true. You are kind of tired.

And the pendulum is swinging so slowly. . . .

Turn to # ***106****.*

#168

The dragon lunges for you. You punch in the numbers 2–4–7 as fast as you can. You hope you got it right!

Just as the beast's huge maw is about to swallow you, a terrible groan fills the castle. It sounds like an earthquake!

The dragon screams, but the sound fades as the monster breaks into a thousand little parts.

Rocks fall from the ceiling. You put your hands over your head and close your eyes.

When you open them, you can't believe what you see.

Turn to # ***107****.*

#169

What? You're going to face the Visible Man with nothing but your bare hands?

Are you crazy?

Explore this floor for something to fight him with.

After all, *anything* is better than nothing!

Check out the map on # ***205****. Then turn to #* ***194****.*

#170

You reach your hand nervously into the spinning wheels and gears.

The mechanism of the machine churns all around your hand. You swallow with a dry throat, hoping nothing catches you.

Some of those gears look sharp!

Can you grab the computer? Roll to find out.

If you're wearing long sleeves, subtract one from your roll.

If you roll 7 or higher, go to # ***5****.*

If you roll 6 or lower, go to # ***109****.*

#171

You decide that the idea is just too risky.

But you do spot something that might be useful later.

There's an exhibit about how wings work. And in the glass case is a real Australian boomerang!

If you take it, write *Boomerang* on your inventory list.

Cool. But what's that buzzing sound behind you?

---

*Turn to # **108**.*

#172

You bend down and shove at the base of the Tesla coil.

The static electricity gets stronger. The hairs on your neck stand up. You feel as if spiders were walking all over you.

And for some reason the lightning bolts are getting bigger!

Then lightning leaps from one of the antennae. You fall back. The bolt just misses you!

Another bolt of lightning shoots out. And another.

You take off. But will the next bolt hit you?

Can you escape the lightning? Roll to find out.

*If you roll 8 or higher, go to # **204**.*

*If you roll 7 or lower, go to # **90**.*

#173

You decide to head east.

You approach the glow very carefully. In this place, it could be anything!

You go about thirty paces east, then turn south again. In only ten paces, you reach a small room.

"Excellent!" you shout when you see what's there.

A laser! Just what Peedee A. said you needed to show the Visible Man a thing or two!

But then you notice what else is in the room.

Turn to # ***236***.

#174

You grasp the controls and nudge the plane closer to the runway. Then you spot a sign. It flashes: LOWER LANDING GEAR.

Good idea!

You find the right button and push it. You settle your plane down, softly as a feather.

When you open the door, you're covered with sweat. That's kind of silly. It was just a simulation, after all.

"Great landing!" a voice on the radio pronounces.

It sounds like your pal Peedee A.!

Turn to # ***26***.

#175

You leap down the stairs. You can barely keep your balance in the rushing water. A huge wave roars behind you, big enough to crush you.

But the door to the first floor is right in front of you. You fling it open and shut it behind you just in time. The water crashes against it, but then flows on down into the basement.

You made it!

There, about a hundred yards away, is the main entrance to the hall. Escape is right in front of you!

Except for one *big* problem.

Turn to # ***126****.*

#176

You dash for the door out of Aerodynamics. But the giant mosquito overtakes you. It descends in front of you, blocking your way out.

It moves toward you. The hideous bloodsucking tube is only a few feet away.

You've got to get away from it!

But how?

Jump into the flight simulator? Turn to # ***233****.*

Try to run past the mosquito and out the door? Turn to # ***65****.*

#177

You stop running and lift the laser to your shoulder.

You aim the red light of the laser at the dinosaur's face. "Take this, fossil-breath!" you shout.

But the creature keeps clanking toward you.

You gulp as you suddenly realize something.

The skeleton doesn't have eyes. The laser can't blind it as it did the Visible Man!

The gigantic skeleton towers over you, reaching for you with its foot-long teeth. Looks like it's . . .

GAME OVER.

#178

The mosquito zooms at you, fast and furious. But finally it makes one mistake. It zips in too close, and your fire extinguisher connects with it.

WHACK!

Ewwwwwww! Mosquito guts everywhere.

"Got you!" you cheer.

Congratulations. This is definitely the biggest bug you've ever squashed.

Turn to # ***159***.

#179

You glance around the Thinking Machines Room.

Hmmm. Old-fashioned computers, regular ones, and futuristic ones.

Which should you take a closer look at?

---

*The old calculating machines? Turn to # **147**.*

*The regular computers? Turn to # **62**.*

*The futuristic computers? Turn to # **232**.*

*Leave the Thinking Machines Room? Go back to # **161**.*

#180

You barely grasp the cable. A scream bursts out of you as you dangle over the black elevator shaft. You swing once, twice, and hurl yourself back toward the doorway.

You land with just an inch to spare.

You take in a shaky breath. You're going to have to be very careful here in the hall. Even the building is out to get you.

How are you going to get out of here?

---

*If you haven't found a phone, search for one now. Turn to # **89**.*

*If you've already tried the phone, turn to # **220** and check out the map.*

#181

You run as fast as you can. The doors are almost within reach. You've made it!

But when you pull the handles, they don't budge. Locked!

You turn and face the lumbering skeleton. Maybe you can make it back to the stairway doors.

Can you make it back to the stairway doors? Roll to find out. By now you're pretty tired. And all the stuff you're carrying is weighing you down. For every object on your inventory list, subtract one from your roll.

If you roll 6 or higher, go to # ***3****.*

If you roll 5 or lower, go to # ***42****.*

#182

You decide to make a smoke bomb. Maybe you can sneak past the Visible Man under a cloud of thick smoke.

You follow the directions carefully. But when you're done, something strange starts to happen.

The chemicals bubble and smoke. They're going crazy!

Maybe someone changed the directions, you think — just before the mixture explodes in a cloud of poisonous fumes.

Guess your idea went up in a puff of smoke!

GAME OVER

#183

You carefully pull the glove from the space suit.

It comes off with a *SNAP*. You slide your hand into it.

Write *Space Glove* on your inventory list.

Then you whirl at a terrible scraping sound behind you.

Turn to # ***231***.

#184

The gloves reach down and pick up a stone, pulling your hands with them. You can't help yourself!

"Right over there," the dragon instructs, pointing a claw.

You try to resist, but it's useless.

"Hurry up, now," the dragon roars. "If you finish this one quickly, maybe I'll let you build another! It should only take about a hundred years. . . ."

As the dragon's laughter echoes through the virtual hills, you find yourself reaching for another rock.

Well, this ending puts the "drag" back in "dragon"!

GAME OVER

#185

You try to fight to stay awake, but the soothing voice is lulling you to sleep.

That's okay. You're tired, very tired.

You just want to stand here. Stand here while the pendulum swings closer and closer.

After all, those spikes are kind of pretty.

Soon, they'll reach you. And you'll get a long, long rest.

Because this is . . .

GAME OVER!

#186

You peer down.

The robot arm! It caught up to you. And now it's clutching your foot in its metal claw. It hoists you up into the air.

The helicopters swarm around you as you dangle upside down.

Then they move in closer.

And closer . . .

Ouch!

Now you know why they call them choppers!

GAME OVER

(Here's a hint: You need the boomerang to beat the robot arm. The boomerang is somewhere on this floor.)

You cautiously peer around the Thinking Machines Room.

It's full of computers and calculating machines. Some are over a hundred years old, big mechanical devices that must weigh a ton.

Some are regular computers, like the ones you use in school.

Others have cool helmets and gloves instead of screens and keyboards. They almost seem to be from the future.

It was one of the regular computers that sent you the message that started all this.

Which ones should you take a closer look at?

The old calculating machines? Turn to # ***147****.*

The regular computers? Turn to # ***62****.*

The futuristic computers? Turn to # ***232****.*

Leave the Thinking Machines Room? Go back to # ***161****.*

#188

You wrench your hand from the door. The effort throws you back onto the floor. You clutch your tingling fingers.

This whole building is a booby trap!

So how are you going to get out?

You suppose you could try the elevator again. But will it do you any good? You know the Super Computer controls it.

Maybe, instead, you should search for a way to open the door without getting fried.

Which will it be?

Search for a way to open the door? Turn to # ***67***.

Try the elevator again? Turn to # ***131***.

#189

At the base of the bulb is a big light switch!

Should you flick the switch? Maybe the light will go out and the bulb will cool off enough to climb on top of it.

Or should you run for the door?

Flick the switch? Turn to # ***165***.

Run for the door? Turn to # ***137***.

#190

You decide to go back to the fire stairs.

You've got to face the Visible Man sooner or later!

As you walk up to the doors, you gulp. He's still banging on them from the other side.

He sure doesn't give up easily!

You ready yourself to open the doors.

Choose your weapon. But remember, you can only use an object that's on your inventory list!

Stink bomb? Turn to # ***114****.*

Noise bomb? Turn to # ***2****.*

Laser? Turn to # ***51****.*

No weapon? Turn to # ***169****.*

#191

You walk over to the Tesla coil.

As you get closer, your hair stands on end.

But not because you're scared. It's just the static electricity from the big coil. There's a zapping noise every time the lightning bolts travel up the antenna.

Hmmm. Maybe you could use it to zap the Giganotosaurus.

Can you move the coil?

Or should you check out the electric toys?

Move the Tesla coil? Turn to # ***172****.*

Examine the electric toys instead? Turn to # ***74****.*

#192

A flock of model helicopters is flying toward you!

They swarm out of the Aerodynamics Room. They're only about two feet across, but there are a dozen of them. And those propeller blades look sharp!

"Why is everything here out to get me?" you wail.

Should you fly for the stairway door? Or maybe hit the ground and take cover?

What'll it be?

Fly for the stairway door? Turn to # ***140****.*

Take cover on the ground? Turn to # ***235****.*

You decide to check out the Waves and Motion Room.

You enter the large room and discover displays about light waves, sound waves, even ocean waves. And the map said there was a laser in here. That would make a good weapon.

Unfortunately, you don't spot any laser. All you see is a sign that says:

TO GET TO THE GIANT MAGNET, THE PENDULUM, AND THE LASER, GO THROUGH THE MAZE OF MIRRORS.

The Maze of Mirrors fills most of the room. You peek in.

It's like an amusement park fun house, with lots of mirrors reflecting into infinity. You gulp. It would be pretty easy to get lost in there.

Are you up to the challenge?

Leave the room? Turn to # ***194****.*

If you want to enter the Maze of Mirrors, check to see if you have the compass on your list.

Enter the maze with the compass? Turn to # ***138****.*

Enter the maze with no compass? Turn to # ***75****.*

(Here's a hint: The compass is in the gift shop.)

#194

There are five places you can get to from here.

One is the elevator, which you aren't sure you can trust.

There's also the fire stairs. They lead down to the rest of the Hall of Incredible Science. And to the Visible Man. . . .

There's a room called the Wonder of Life. Hmmm.

And another room called Waves and Motion.

There's also a gift shop. Maybe you'll find some useful stuff there. If you can get in there, that is.

Where do you want to go?

Try the fire stairs? Turn to # ***190****.*

Try the elevator? Turn to # ***38****.*

The Wonder of Life Room? Turn to # ***216****.*

The Waves and Motion Room? Turn to # ***193****.*

The gift shop? Turn to # ***141****.*

#195

You try to pull off the visor. But for some reason your hands won't move. It's as if the gloves were fighting back!

The dragon laughs again.

"You're in *my* universe now!" it rumbles. "What makes you think you can just come and go as you please?"

A moment later, the chamber starts to dissolve around you.

All right! Maybe the computer is running down!

But when you see what happens next, you realize that luck isn't with you today.

Turn to # ***215***.

#196

"Where do I find that? Over," you ask.

"Check the map of the third floor," Peedee A. responds. "Got to go now. Over and out."

"Over and out," you mutter. You're glad Peedee A. is helping you. But you wish he — or she, or it — wouldn't keep fading out on you. You'd like a little company in this creepy place!

You tuck the walkie-talkie into your backpack. Write *Walkie-talkie* on your inventory list.

Before you head out, you take a last look around.

Something really interesting catches your eye.

Turn to # ***98***.

#197

You sprint for the door, leaping over the little dinosaurs before they really get going.

But as you run, you hear their wheels starting to turn. They're coming after you!

You make it to the door just a few feet ahead of them.

But will they follow you out?

Turn to # ***99***.

#198

You decide to use the noise bomb. That should give this slithery snake a scare!

You toss the red jar into the air and cover your ears.

KABOOOOOOOOM!

The snake *must* be stunned after a blast like that.

But as you reach for the laser, the serpent strikes!

As your arms and legs grow stiff, you remember that snakes can't hear. They don't even have ears. So it's . . .

GAME OVER.

(Here's a hint: You'll need a bomb to scare off the snake. But not a noise bomb.)

#199

You try to stop yourself, but your feet are dangling above the ground. There's nothing you can do. The copters carry you out of the Aerodynamics Room and up toward the ceiling.

The whine of their little blades grows stronger and stronger. You're going *way* too fast.

You're headed for the skylight!

CRASH!

---

*Turn to # **82**.*

#200

As you hit the red button, a hissing sound starts.

Then a computer voice declares, "Launch sequence activated. Fifteen seconds and counting."

You wildly push the other buttons, but none of them do anything.

"Ten. Nine. Eight . . ."

You gulp. Maybe the red button wasn't such a good idea.

---

*Turn to # **18**.*

#201

You clear your throat.

"You're the Super Computer, aren't you?" you ask, trying to sound bold.

The dragon rears to its full height. It stares down at you as if you were an insect.

"I am that, and much more!" it roars. "I have taken over the Hall of Incredible Science. And soon I will take over the world!"

Wow! This is one nutty computer! But maybe it will listen to reason.

"Uh — since you're going to take over the world anyway, maybe you could let *me* go," you suggest meekly.

Turn to # ***163****.*

#202

You walk ten paces north, then turn back toward the west.

Thirty paces later, you reach a junction. You've been here before!

You can head north or south. . . .

Which will it be?

North? Turn to # ***214****.*
South? Turn to # ***224****.*

#203

You hold the fire extinguisher in front of you like a club. “Come and get me, bloodsucker!” you shout.

The mosquito zips toward you, but each time you swing the extinguisher, it flits out of reach.

It attacks again and again, trying to stick you with its bloodsucking tube. But you manage to fend it off.

Who will win this fight to the death?

Can you beat the mosquito? Roll to find out.

If you roll 6 or higher, go to # ***77****.*

If you roll 5 or lower, go to # ***178****.*

#204

As you run, another bolt leaps from the coil.

Whoa! That was close!

By now you’re out of range. A few more bolts flash out, but they can’t reach you.

Gradually, the coil returns to normal.

You sigh with relief.

Maybe you should stick to something less electrifying!

Check out the electric toys? Turn to # ***74****.*

Or leave the Electricity Room? Turn to # ***13****.*

#205

This map shows the third floor.

You quickly sketch it into your notebook for later use. If you ever need to refer to it again, turn back to # 205.

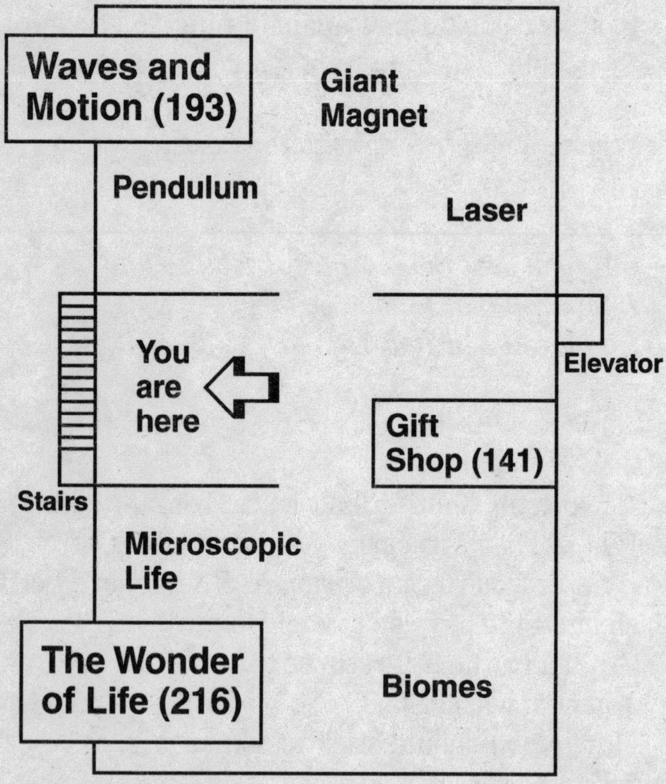

Write down "MAP OF 3rd FLOOR AT # 205." But when you come here to glance at the map, make sure to remember where you came from.

If this is your first time here, turn to # ***194****.*

#206

He opens his mouth to speak. His voice sounds watery, like someone gargling while he talks. You stare in terrified fascination as his visible vocal cords move.

"I told you that you couldn't escape," he gurgles.

It's the voice of the Super Computer!

The Visible Man reaches toward you.

What should you do?

Duck into the third floor, or run past him?

Run past him? Turn to # ***228****.*

Duck into the third floor? Turn to # ***54****.*

#207

You decide to check out the Aerodynamics Room.

"Cool," you murmur as you enter. There are model aircraft everywhere. And models of birds and other flying creatures.

There's also a big flight simulator like the ones pilots train in. Hey! Maybe it has a radio like a real plane, you think. I could use it to call for help.

What should you check out first?

The model aircraft? Turn to # ***213****.*

Or maybe the model birds? Turn to # ***31****.*

Give the flight simulator a test flight? Turn to # ***52****.*

Leave the room? Turn to # ***166****.*

#208

You decide to go east.

You walk ten paces. Then the hall turns south.

After twenty paces south, you have to turn east again.

You walk twenty more paces east, to a junction.

You can go north or south. Which will it be?

North? Turn to # ***154***.
South? Turn to # ***40***.

#209

You approach the suit cautiously.

"It's me, Peedee A.," the suit declares. "I'm using the radio in the space helmet."

"You scared me!" you grumble.

"Sorry," Peedee A. apologizes. "Listen, I have to talk fast. The Super Computer was controlling the robot arm. When you switched off the arm, you froze the computer."

"You mean I beat it?" you cry. "Yes!"

"No, no," Peedee A. says impatiently. "It's just rebooting. It will be back. Listen! Now that you've got the space glove, you can get down the fire stairs without getting electrocuted by the handle. But watch out for the —"

A hiss of static drowns out the voice.

Turn to # ***229***.

#210

You decide to make a noise bomb.

You follow the directions carefully, mixing chemicals in a little test tube. You wind up with a jar of red goo.

You're very careful as you screw on the metal cap. If it breaks — *KABOOOOM!*

Write *Noise Bomb* on your inventory list.

You leave the gift shop, smiling. It's about time you did some of the scaring around here!

Turn to # ***194***.

#211

You stare out the front window. The scene appears to be rolling forward.

You're moving!

Can't be, you assure yourself. This is just a simulation.

The end of the runway is coming up. You grab the controls. Maybe this flight isn't real, but you're not taking any chances.

Then the voice comes on again.

"Emergency! Emergency! There is a giant mosquito — repeat, a giant mosquito — on the wing! Execute Emergency Maneuver 6-Q!"

6-Q? You wonder what that is.

Then the plane starts to pitch sideways.

Turn to # ***71***.

#212

You climb the wet stairs back to the second floor.

You sigh. Escape seemed so close. But now you're headed back to another floor of the hall.

Maybe you can find something to help you fight the giant skeleton. Or maybe you'll find another way out.

You open the door to the second floor cautiously. In front of you is another map.

Great!

But when you see what's on it, a cold shiver of fear runs down your spine. . . .

Turn to # ***23***.

#213

You walk over to the model aircraft.

In addition to planes, you spot blimps, helicopters, even hang gliders. Too bad they're just models. Otherwise you could hang glide out of this crazy hall.

But that gives you an idea. . . .

Maybe if you got all the helicopters working together, they could lift you! You could fly out a window and all the way home!

What do you think?

Think it's a stupid, crazy idea? Turn to # ***171***.
Give it a shot? Turn to # ***222***.

#214

You decide to head north.

The long, mirrored hallway goes sixty paces north. Then it turns west and goes another sixty paces.

Finally, you reach another junction. You can head south or keep going west.

Listening carefully, you hear a swooshing sound from the west. It sounds like a giant blade swinging back and forth!

Your stomach flip-flops.

Which way should you go?

West? Turn to # ***20***.

South? Turn to # ***146***.

#215

Walls of stone appear around you. There's only one tiny window in the room. And no door.

You're in a dungeon!

You try to move your hands, but they're paralyzed. The virtual reality gloves are like shackles on your wrists.

The dragon's voice comes through the tiny window.

"Welcome to your new home," it booms. "I hope you like it. You're going to be here for a long, long time."

The dragon's laughter fades as it stomps away.

It looks as if virtual reality is your only reality now!

GAME OVER

#216

You decide to go to the Wonder of Life Room. Maybe there's something in there that will help you fight the Visible Man.

As you enter, you gulp.

Right next to the door is a big display labeled THE VISIBLE MAN. But, of course, the man himself is missing.

There are two sections in the room. Microscopic Life and something called "Biomes."

Where should you go?

---

*Check out Microscopic Life? Turn to # **157**.*

*Or Biomes — whatever those are? Turn to # **83**.*

#217

As you pull back on the controls, the windshield fills with blue sky. You're pressed into your seat. Wow! It feels so *real*.

But you have no time to enjoy the flight.

"Fire in Number Two engine," the voice warns.

"What do I do?" you cry.

The voice suddenly changes to an evil laugh.

"I'm afraid I can't help you," it cackles.

You've heard that voice before. It's the Super Computer!

You gulp. What should you do?

---

*Keep flying? Turn to # **44**.*

*Try to land? Turn to # **12**.*

#218

"It's me, Peedee A.," the message reads. "You're very close to me now. I'm trapped in the difference engine. If you help me escape, I can show you how to defeat the Super Computer."

Wow! You've almost found your pal Peedee A.!

You peer around, wondering what a "difference engine" is.

Where should you start looking?

The old calculating machines? Turn to # ***147***.

The futuristic computers? Turn to # ***232***.

Leave the Thinking Machines Room? Go back to # ***161***.

#219

You decide to head east.

After a few moments of walking you hear the sound of several people approaching.

Maybe it's a rescue party!

"Hey!" you cry. "Help!"

It turns out to be a troop of Nature Scouts. They've been lost in the Maze of Mirrors for two years!

Unfortunately, you and the Nature Scouts never escape the Hall of Incredible Science. But after a few more years, you earn enough merit badges to achieve the rank of Acorn.

Congratulations! But . . .

GAME OVER!

This map shows the fourth floor.

You quickly sketch it into your notebook for later use. If you ever need to refer to it again, turn back to # 220.

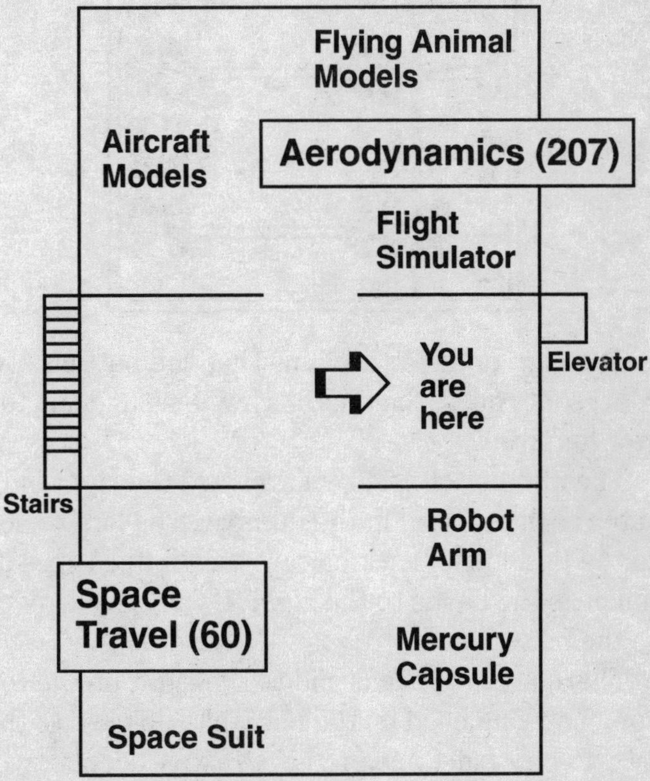

Write down "MAP OF 4th FLOOR AT # 220." But when you come here to glance at the map, make sure to remember where you came from.

If this is your first time here, turn to # ***166****.*

#221

The PDA told you the Crash Code might be on the abacus. With the code, you can turn off the Super Computer — permanently!

The abacus looks like this:

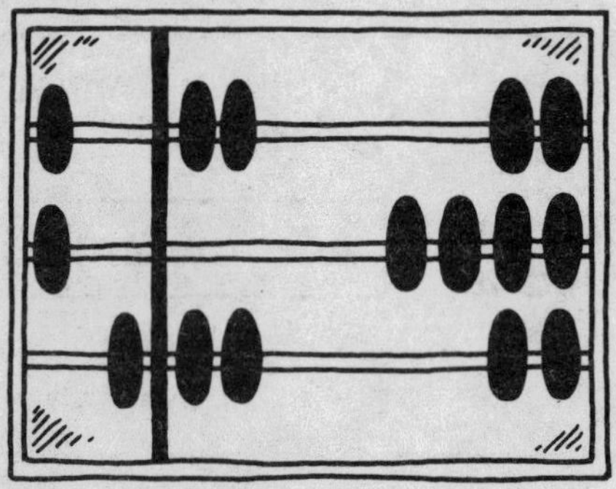

The sign under it explains that the bottom row represents ones, the middle row tens, and the top row hundreds.

The number of beads slid toward the right indicates each numeral in the number. The lone beads to the left of the black bar are worth five times as much as the beads to the right, if they're slid over to the bar.

There are two beads slid to the right on the top row. The lone bead on the left isn't slid over to the bar. "That must mean the Crash Code is two-hundred-and-something," you mutter. "I *think*."

Too bad math isn't your best subject.

Can you read the rest of the abacus? If you can, write down the Crash Code. You'll need it later.

When you've solved the abacus, turn to # ***179****.*

#222

"It just might work!" you mutter.

You find the remote control for the helicopters.

But how are you going to attach yourself? You spot an exhibit on parachutes. The parachute in the glass case seems kind of old, but the harness is in good shape.

You slip into the harness. You tie the ropes to the model helicopters.

Then you push the start button, and gulp. . . .

---

*Turn to # **145**.*

#223

You approach the space suit. It's wearing a jet pack like the kind astronauts use in space.

The suit is old and dusty and much bigger than you.

You sure hope it's really empty!

One of the space gloves seems loose. Hey. A big glove like that could come in handy for touching dangerous things.

What do you think?

---

*Take the space glove? Turn to # **183**.*
*Check out the capsule instead? Turn to # **148**.*
*Leave the Space Travel Room? Back to # **166**.*

#224

You decide to head south.

Only thirty paces later, you reach another junction.

You can go further south or head to the west.

Which way?

West? Turn to # ***115****.*
South? Turn to # ***40****.*

#225

Climbing on top of the giant lightbulb seems to be your best bet.

You race toward the huge bulb. The glare almost blinds you. The little motors of the dinosaurs whir as they chase you.

You jump toward the bulb.

Ouch! You jerk back. It's as hot as a stove!

You swallow nervously as the dinos close in.

But then you notice something that gives you hope.

Turn to # ***189****.*

#226

"This space glove is in my way," you mutter. You throw it down and quickly unstrap the jet pack from the space suit.

From behind you comes the terrifying scrape of the robot arm dragging itself toward you.

In seconds, you've strapped yourself in. You push a button on the jet pack. You just hope it's the right one.

The robot arm reaches for you. Its metal claw glints in the jet pack's fiery exhaust. But you lift off, out of its reach.

You're flying!

Turn to # ***55***.

#227

As you enter the Electricity Room, it fills with light. The light comes from a huge bulb standing right in the middle of the room. Along the walls are electric cars, electric toys, even little electric models of the big dinosaur downstairs.

But the weirdest thing is a huge coil like a TV antenna, with lightning bolts rising up between the two rods every few seconds. Something a mad scientist might have. The label underneath it says TESLA COIL.

Then a strange thing happens.

Turn to # ***132***.

#228

You're pretty good at dodgeball. You decide to try to run past the Visible Man.

You leap onto the handrail of the stairs. In an instant, you're sliding quickly downward.

You're going to make it!

Turn to # ***7***.

#229

"Watch out for what?" you demand.

"Super Computer . . . coming back," Peedee A. shouts over the static. "Watch out . . . Visible Man . . ."

Then the static switches off, and another voice comes through. Loud and clear.

"You've won this round," it roars. "But you'll never escape! Ha, ha, ha!"

The Super Computer's laughter rings out as you turn and run.

Turn to # ***64***.

#230

You decide to head east.

You follow the corridor for thirty paces. Then it turns north.

Ten paces later, you find yourself at another junction. You hear a humming from the north.

You can keep going north or you can turn east.

Which way?

North? Turn to # ***25***.
East? Turn to # ***208***.

#231

You gasp. The robot arm — it's moving!

It's reaching out and grabbing the floor. Dragging itself toward you. In a few more seconds, it'll be able to grab *you*.

You don't think it wants to shake hands.

Should you try to run around it? It has an awfully long reach!

Or maybe you could use the jet pack from the space suit to escape.

What should you do? Think fast!

Run past the robot arm? Turn to # ***81***.
Use the jet pack? Turn to # ***15***.
If you have the boomerang, turn to # ***133***.

#232

You decide you're ready for the futuristic computers.

They are totally cool!

Instead of screens and keyboards, they have visors and gloves. You put them on. The world you see inside the visors is completely generated by the computers.

The sign over the exhibit reads A TICKET TO VIRTUAL REALITY.

You just hope it's not a one-way ticket!

Put on the gloves and visor? Turn to # ***16***.

Check out the rest of the room? Turn to # ***179***.

Leave the Thinking Machines Room? Turn to # ***161***.

#233

You hurl yourself into the simulator and slam the door shut. The mosquito buzzes angrily against the small window.

You're safe. For now.

You glance around. The inside of the simulator is just like the cockpit of a huge jetliner. A million controls and readouts and two big chairs.

Then a tinny voice announces, "Flight 13, you are ready for takeoff."

Takeoff?

Turn to # ***211***.

#234

You decide to throw the boomerang at the mosquito.

The giant insect is right in front of you. You can't miss!

You cock back your arm and throw as hard as you can.

The mosquito flits to one side.

Okay, so you *can* miss.

At least the boomerang is coming back. You can try again.

If the mosquito doesn't get you first. . . .

---

*Turn to # **135**.*

#235

You turn off the jet pack and fall to the ground.

The spinning blades of the little helicopters whiz just over your head. You duck.

But there's another one — coming straight at you. Low enough to chop you to bits!

You try to roll out of the way.

Can you escape the helicopter? Roll to find out.

*If you roll 7 or higher, go to # **37**.*

*If you roll 6 or lower, go to # **110**.*

#236

Coiled around the laser is a long black snake!

Its tongue flicks out at you. You spot its long, curving fangs. They drip with something that looks like poison.

You take a quick survey of your possessions. Which of them will work against this deadly opponent? Remember, you can only use something that's on your inventory list.

The space glove? Turn to # ***144****.*
The fire extinguisher? Turn to # ***14****.*
A stink bomb? Turn to # ***111****.*
A noise bomb? Turn to # ***198****.*
Slink back out of the room? Turn to # ***136****.*

#237

A new voice takes over the walkie-talkie.

The Super Computer!

"Very clever, human," it booms. "But I'm not done yet!"

"Oh, yeah?" you shout. "I'm winning so far!"

"Let's see you win against this!" the voice roars.

Water suddenly starts spraying from the ceiling. It gushes from the sprinklers above, soaking you.

"Hah!" you laugh. "A little water never hurt anyone."

But then you hear a rushing sound building above you.

It sounds like more than just a *little* water.

---

*Turn to # **27**.*

#238

You land at a stone temple in the middle of a jungle.

Hey, you recognize this scene. It's from your favorite movie, *Operation Buzzard.* Stagehands rush by, carrying props.

"They're filming the sequel," the PDA explains.

"Wow!" you exclaim. "Does this mean I get to meet my all-time favorite movie star, Terry Thomas?"

"In a way," the PDA answers. She hands you a mirror.

You stare into it. Hey! That's not your face.

It's the face of Terry Thomas!

"But how — how —" you sputter.

The PDA grins. "It's virtual reality, remember? You can be anyone you want! Now, are you ready for the first scene?"

"I guess so," you reply. Wow! This is so excellent!

"And . . . action!" the director calls.

A rumbling sound fills the air. Glancing up, you spot an elephant charging toward you. Uh-oh! What should you do?

Suddenly, you realize you never read the script.

Looks like you'll have to wing it. You glance around. You could grab a vine and try to swing to safety — or you could . . .

"Oh, no," you groan. "Here we go again!"

THE END

About R.L. Stine

R.L. STINE is the most popular author in America. He is the creator of the *Goosebumps*, *Give Yourself Goosebumps*, *Fear Street*, and *Ghosts of Fear Street* series, among other popular books. He has written more than 100 scary novels for kids. Bob lives in New York City with his wife, Jane, teenage son, Matt, and dog, Nadine.

SHE'S NOT GOING TO GIVE YOU
DETENTION.
SHE'S NOT GOING TO GIVE YOU
A BAD GRADE.
SHE'S GOING TO
EAT YOU.
Goosebumps
SERIES 2000
R.L. STINE
Book #3: Creature Teacher
The next millennium will shock you.
In bookstores this February.
Copyright © 1997 by Parachute Press, Inc. GOOSEBUMPS is a registered trademark of Parachute Press, Inc. All rights reserved. GBT797
SCHOLASTIC
PARACHUT

❑ BAB56888-4	#51	Beware, the Snowman	
❑ BAB56889-2	#52	How I Learned to Fly	
❑ BAB56890-6	#53	Chicken Chicken	
❑ BAB56891-4	#54	Don't Go to Sleep!	
❑ BAB56892-2	#55	The Blob That Ate Everyone	
❑ BAB56893-0	#56	The Curse of Camp Cold Lake	
❑ BAB56894-9	#57	My Best Friend Is Invisible	
❑ BAB56895-7	#58	Deep Trouble II	
❑ BAB56897-3	#59	The Haunted School	
❑ BAB39053-8	#60	Werewolf Skin	
❑ BAB39986-1	#61	I Live in Your Basement!	
❑ BAB39987-X	#62	Monster Blood IV	
❑ BAB35007-2		Goosebumps Triple Header Book #1	$3.99
❑ BAB62836-4		Tales to Give You Goosebumps Book & Light Set Special Edition #1	$11.95
❑ BAB48993-3		Tales to Give You Goosebumps Special Edition #1	$3.99
❑ BAB26603-9		More Tales to Give You Goosebumps Book & Light Set Special Edition #2	$11.95
❑ BAB26002-0		More Tales to Give You Goosebumps Special Edition #2	$3.99
❑ BAB74150-4		Even More Tales to Give You Goosebumps Book and Boxer Shorts Pack Special Edition #3	$14.99
❑ BAB73909-3		Even More Tales to Give You Goosebumps Special Edition #3	$3.99
❑ BAB88132-9		Still More Tales to Give You Goosebumps Scare Pack Special Edition #4	$11.95
❑ BAB23795-0		More and More Tales to Give You Goosebumps Book and Cap Pack Special Edition #5	$11.95
❑ BAB34119-7		Goosebumps Fright Light Edition	$12.95
❑ BAB36682-3		More & More & More Tales to Give You Goosebumps Special Edition #6 Book and Holiday Stocking Set	$9.95
❑ BAB53770-9		The Goosebumps Monster Blood Pack	$11.95
❑ BAB50995-0		The Goosebumps Monster Edition #1	$12.95
❑ BAB93371-X		The Goosebumps Monster Edition #2	$12.95
❑ BAB36673-4		The Goosebumps Monster Edition #3	$12.95
❑ BAB60265-9		The Goosebumps Official Collector's Caps Collecting Kit	$5.99
❑ BAB73906-9		The Goosebumps Postcard Book	$7.95
❑ BAB31259-6		The Goosebumps Postcard Book II	$7.95
❑ BAB32717-8		The 1998 Goosebumps 365 Scare-a-Day Calendar	$8.95
❑ BAB10485-3		The Goosebumps 1998 Wall Calendar	$10.99

Scare me, thrill me, mail me GOOSEBUMPS now!

Available wherever you buy books, or use this order form.
Scholastic Inc., P.O. Box 7502, Jefferson City, MO 65102

Please send me the books I have checked above. I am enclosing $____________ (please add $2.00 to cover shipping and handling). Send check or money order—no cash or C.O.D.s please.

Name ______________________________ Age ____________

Address ____

City ______________________________ State/Zip ____________

Please allow four to six weeks for delivery. Offer good in the U.S. only. Sorry, mail orders are not available to residents of Canada. Prices subject to change.

GB597